HIS
FORBIDDEN
OMEGA

THE ROYAL OMEGAS
BOOK ONE

P. JAMESON
KRISTEN STRASSEL

HIS FORBIDDEN OMEGA

Copyright © 2019 by P. Jameson
and Kristen Strassel

First electronic publication: August 2019
United States of America

ISBN: 9781694632982

First Digital Publication: August 2019
First Print Publication: September 2019

Cover Design: Sotia Lazu
Formatting: Agent X Graphics

PJAMESONBOOKS.COM
KRISTENSTRASSEL.COM

ONE
KING ADALAI

Another battle was won. Another enemy trampled under my watch. And the excitement it bred in my blood was like a drug I never wanted free of.

I stomped to my balcony, stepping into the night and threw my clenched fists into the air in triumph as I looked down at my people crowding the streets below. The rumble of a fierce growl grew in my chest until it exploded from my throat, vicious and inhuman. And the resulting thunderous roar from below told me the others were drunk on victory too.

I

Tonight, there would be much fucking.

Tomorrow, there would be a celebration. A feast worthy of a king and his court, to show the people of Luxoria their leader was powerful enough to bring down the great humans who wanted to capture and study them.

For the first time in too long I, King Adalai of the Weren, was deserving of my place on the throne.

I was alpha. I was powerful. I owned the fucking ground my people walked on.

And unlike my father, no one would ever take it away from me.

I turned back to the meeting room where my closest advisors awaited my command.

"Report," I growled, pacing the floor. My cock was hard from the battle. Only killing made it this way. I'd need a female tonight. Perhaps a curvy beta to knot in. I would have one brought to me after business was complete.

Evander, Solen, Cassian, and Dagger stood, bloody fists clenching, chests rumbling just like mine. Each of them an alpha in their own right, they likely needed to rut away the battle just as I did.

We'd make this quick.

"The troops came at us from all sides, including the south," Evander announced.

"The south. They approached the Badlands?" The territory to the south was reserved for the omega shifters. Those who were banished after The Division. And it was a dead barren waste.

Dagger, who was in charge of the south, nodded. "A mistake of course. The omegas had them on the run before the royal forces even arrived."

"Losses?" I asked.

"A mere eight from the east," Solen practically roared.

"Twelve from the west." Cassien grinned, his eyes flashing dark with bloodlust. "But ask me how many we took down. Because that number is much more impressive."

Evander growled a warning. "Four from the

3

North," he said. "Two of them younglings who were coming into their alpha year."

A shame. But the ones weak enough to die weren't strong enough for the pack.

I looked to Dagger. I already knew his number but I waited for him to answer anyhow.

"Zero from the Badlands." He looked satisfied. "The omegas grow stronger even as they grow weaker."

Which shouldn't make the sick bastard happy at all. But Dagger wasn't normal. It was what made him perfect for policing the Badlands.

I looked around at my men. What was normal anyway?

We were royalty, but we weren't refined.

We weren't proper, and certainly not civil. But we were better than the filth that lived beyond the gates in the Badlands. We had technology that kept us fed and living in lush green land. Kept water flowing through our city. We had factories where omegas labored to produce the finest clothing and furniture and artillery. We had entertainment, soft beds, and all our hearts desired at the snap of a fucking finger.

But it was all a grand scheme. A costume we wore.

Because inside, we were all beasts.

And it was no more evident than it was on the battlefield where we crushed our human enemies like dried clay in our fists.

Beasts.

Somewhere, deep inside each of us, there was a wolf locked away, unable to find its way out anymore. The ability to shift had been slowly fading away for decades, until the former king—my father—was the only one of us left who could. And for all our godforsaken technology and advancements, no one could seem to figure out why. Eventually even he had succumbed to the hindrance.

Until we were able to shift and be our whole selves, we would never be truly satisfied.

But fighting and fucking and drinking the wine of our people helped ease the sting. So that was how we spent our days and nights.

It was an empty existence but it was better than beyond the gates. Better than that of the omegas. And the surviving humans we warred with.

"Go," I told my men. "Find betas to warm your beds. You deserve them. Tomorrow, we celebrate."

Nodding, they filed out, wordlessly.

Strolling to the bar, I loosened my groin-cloak and let it fall to the stone floor, giving my cock the room it needed. It jutted out before me hard and aching and unrelenting. The throbbing bulb at the end assured me it was too far gone to go away on its own. And the idea of taking a beta to bed again... didn't leave me breathless.

I poured a goblet of wine and brought it to my lips, savoring the rich flavor before crossing the room to sit on the lush couch that my beta squire insisted I have. It was rather comfortable, but it didn't bring me the comfort I needed.

The kingdom my father and others had built

was under constant threat. And the sa.
rested solely on my shoulders now. I was n.
Alpha.

Others wanted that title and fought me for it
often.

If I was any less of a male, I would give it to
them and laugh as I strode away, knowing the sort
of pressure they would then face.

But I was not a lowly male.

I was the fiercest male in the pack. Even if I
had to constantly prove it.

That's the way you keep the throne. My
father's words were always and forever in my
mind.

Sipping my wine, I thought of the omegas that
lived outside the city and what Dagger's report
meant. *They grow stronger even as they grow
weaker.*

Once upon a time, omegas lived in the city as
a thriving part of the pack. They were taken as
lovers, treated as friends. Even chosen as queens.
My own mother had been an omega before she

birthed me and became my father's beloved. I wondered what she might've thought of his declaration to let them all die out in the wilderness. Would he still have banished her kind if she'd been around to counsel him?

My mind turned away from thoughts of my mother as I imagined what life was like in the city back then. When we were all one people instead of royals and omegas. Luxoria and the Badlands.

I imagined what it would be like to take an omega under me. To react to her heat, that specific scent the beta females never had. For our hormones to clash and sizzle like our biology was meant to.

The idea was dirty and forbidden.

Unkingly.

Wholly treacherous.

But it made my cock beg for a squeeze of my palm.

And I gave it that, as my thoughts wandered farther.

How different it would be from the beta

couplings I'd had, where there was no instinctive demand to breed. No urge aside from assuaging the hunger to rut. No connection, no burning need.

No scent to drive me mad.

No need to pleasure her again and again, hour after hour, night after night until she was swollen with my baby.

Fuck.

I sucked in a breath finally realizing how my grip had tightened over my swollen knot the same way a female would as she came. I thrust into my fist, furious for a release. Except this time, in my mind, an omega writhed beneath me.

An omega begged me for more, begged me to go harder.

An omega moaned my name.

And when I came, spilling my release all over my hand, it was with a roar of *miiine* to claim my imaginary omega.

When I was drained, out of breath, and limp with pleasure, the realization of what I'd just done struck me like a hammer to the chest.

I fantasized about breeding an omega.

The lowest of lows. The banished traitors of our kind. The ones who made my father crazy in the end.

The reason we fought our wars with the humans.

A dirty fucking omega was in my head.

And it was the best relief I'd had in a long damn time. Maybe ever.

No one could ever know about this.

No one could ever find out about my forbidden hunger.

It was a matter of life or death.

TWO
ZELENE

The old woman behind the table looked nothing like she did before The Division. When I was a little girl, I spent hours in her shop, bored out of my mind while my mother and sister had dresses made. I wasn't allowed to touch any of the beautiful fabrics with colors so vibrant they appealed to every single one of my senses.

I still wasn't allowed to touch the fabrics.

I watched the woman carefully. An omega like me, she'd lost her shop, but she hadn't given up. Those beautiful bolts lay on an open table. The dust from the desert barely dulled their brilliance.

She was little more than a living skeleton now, with her graying skin stretched over gaunt features, and eyes like black holes, reflecting her soul. More like, the spot where her soul should've been. The omegas had lost many things in The Division. But I wouldn't lose that. I would fight tooth and nail to keep my soul intact. No matter the cost.

I moved my gaze to the brilliant bolt of cloth I'd had my eye on, and it was like she sensed my movement.

"Not for you," she snapped. Even in the Badlands, there was a pecking order. Survival demanded respect. The ones who made it happen outside the city had little patience for those of us who worked for the royals. "Unless you're shopping for royalty."

I'd starved myself to buy this fabric. My lie wouldn't make me any more uncomfortable. "I am. My lady needs a dress for the ball."

It wasn't a total lie. I just wouldn't tell her that I was the lady. It would take some getting used to.

In the Badlands, females weren't thought of in those terms. But I dreamed of it, just like I dreamed of turning this fabric into a beautiful dress worthy of a royal ball. All the soft comfort and gentle days that came with commanding such a title. I didn't need to be a queen or a princess. A lady would do.

The old woman wanted money more than she cared about the validity of my story. She picked up the brilliant magenta fabric, gazing at it with much more respect than she held for me. "There's just enough on the bolt to make a dress. The price is six gold coins."

Swallowing my surprise at her number, which was close to what I earned in a year, I reached for the coin purse that I'd secured on the inside of my skirt. The Badlands had yet to establish anything that looked like a real law. Evil wasn't punished. I could grab the bolt of fabric out of her hands and make a run for it. There was nothing she could do to stop me. Just like there was nothing stopping her from calling my bluff and extorting me over pretty fabric.

Quickly, I counted the coins in my purse. I didn't have enough.

"I have silver coins. The equivalent of four gold." It was all the money I had in the world.

She shook her head, hugging the bolt to her body. "A royal would have sent you with gold."

"She gave me silver." Which was partially true. I was paid one silver coin a week. The equivalent of pocket change in the royal city. "Will you deny a royal what they asked for?"

"Come back with gold," she said.

"She gave me silver," I repeated. I expected a negotiation, but when it didn't come, I walked away, disappointed. I'd find another dress to wear to the next castle ball. The fact that an omega like me could be killed for setting foot in said ball was totally irrelevant. I was going.

"Girl." At first, I wasn't sure she meant me, and kept walking. "Girl. I'll take the silver."

The woman gave me a toothless grin as I returned to her table. Anything was better than nothing, every omega in the Badlands knew this.

My hands shook as I gave her the coins. For the next week, I'd only be able to eat when I worked at the castle. If any of the Collectors came to the shack I shared with five other omegas, he'd take his pay however he saw fit.

But for a chance to step into the technicolor life of Luxoria, it was worth it.

The woman lovingly wrapped the brilliant fabric in burlap.

"Did you embroider this yourself?" I asked. "My Lady will want to know."

I prayed she didn't ask who my Lady was. Yes, I worked as a servant, but if I used my access to royalty for my own gain, I could lose my job. Without my job, I'd be left to sell whatever I had on the Badlands open market. I'd die before I joined the ranks of the prostitutes who gave their bodies to the Alphas, hoping for a few copper coins in return. More often than not, the royal men took their fill and gave nothing in return.

The old woman nodded, pride shining

brightly on her face. "Yes. By hand. When I still had a shop."

"She'll appreciate your work," I said.

As the old woman handed me the package, she pulled it back. For a moment, I thought she meant to steal from me. That she intended to keep my coins and my purchase.

"Don't let anyone see you with this until you get to the castle," she said. "They'll think you're claiming to be something you're not, and you will be punished."

"I'll keep it a secret, like my life depends on it." Because it did.

***

"What the hell do you think you're doing?" My sister Tavia stood in the doorway of our shanty, her reflection filling the empty space in the dusty mirror. She was going to get a mouthful of desert dust if she didn't pick up her jaw. "If you get caught in the Lady's dress, you'll be punished."

"It's not the Lady's dress." I might have been a little vague with the details when I said I brought the dress home to work on. I let my sister and the three other women who shared this cramped, dilapidated shack think I'd taken home sewing work to make extra money. Not all of them worked in the castle, but everyone should've been smart enough to know my employers didn't care if I made extra money. "It's mine."

"Zelene," she gasped. "What the hell are you doing?"

"There's a party at the castle tonight to celebrate the latest military victory." I didn't make the dress with this specific party in mind, but in the castle, it seemed like there was always a party. Rooms full of alphas, betas, and royals, all drunk and without a care in the world. As an omega, I'd worked many of them.

Tavia shook her head. "You'll get yourself killed."

Killed. As if I was actually living.

"What is this?" I raised my hands. My dress—hugging my curves with rich magenta and gold—was the most glamorous part of the Badlands.

Daylight shone through the crooked wall slats of our home, and everything was coated with a layer of reddish brown desert dust. It made life in the Badlands one-dimensional, sad, and hopeless. "This isn't living. This is existing. But if I pull this off—"

"You won't." Tavia recently got fired from her job in the castle, no explanation given, no second chances. Now she was scrambling to find something, anything not to fall into the trafficking ring that so many omega women were forced into to survive.

After The Division, omegas were stripped of all shifter rights. Laws that protected the residents of Luxoria no longer applied to us. Rumors swirled that if King Adalai ever shifted into his true wolf form, he might lift his harsh rules on the Badlands. But if omegas knew anything, it was that dreams seldom came true.

Working in the castle had offered us some protection, except for when we faced those who thought our jobs gave us privilege. There was a hierarchy among omegas too. And Tavia was desperate to not fall through the floor straight to the bottom of it.

"Do I look like an omega in this dress?" I challenged.

A wild storm of emotion swirled in her eyes. I knew what it was. Desperation. Exactly why I had to take this chance.

She shook her head, hopeless as ever. "They'll know. They'll see the dust on your skin and hear the rumble in your belly. You're too skinny to be anything but an omega. Your cheeks are too pink from the sun. No dress can hide that."

"After a few glasses of mead, all they'll care about is a place to stick their dick."

Tavia's face paled. She'd been holding secrets from me too. "You know the laws. If anyone in the royal city attempts to mate with an omega, they'll be killed."

I didn't need to mate with just anyone. I needed one male who wasn't an omega, to take notice of me.

"I have to try." I didn't want to cry. I'd put on eye makeup, the little bit I was able to smuggle out of the castle, and I didn't want to mess it up. Tonight, I wasn't an omega. If my plan worked, I could lift up Tavia and all our friends. They could take everything away from me, but I'd tucked my dreams deep in a place where not even the king could reach. "If nothing changes, we'll starve to death, and that's if we're lucky. I'm scared for you, Tavia. I'll do whatever it takes so you don't have to sell yourself night after night."

"That's exactly what you're doing." She clapped her hand over her mouth. Emotion raised the volume of her voice. She knew she couldn't stop me, but she also knew better than to draw attention to herself. "You're selling yourself to someone who doesn't care if we live or die."

"No one cares about us." By design, there was very little loyalty among omegas. We couldn't be a pack without an alpha. The women who lived in this shack did their best to look out for one another. But they'd taken our voices and our power. All we had was comfort and sympathy. We wanted so much more. "I'm willing to take this chance to make our lives better. What if one night could change everything?"

"You always were a dreamer." Tavia's shoulders softened once she realized there was no talking me out of this. No better alternative. She reached into the chest at the end of our bed. The intricately carved mahogany stayed covered in a layer of dust no matter how often we cleaned it, but was the only thing we had left of what belonged to our mom. Everything else we'd been forced to sell to buy food or make rent.

Tavia retrieved one of our everyday dresses from the chest and handed it to me. It was as brown as the dessert. "Put this on until you get to the castle. Don't draw attention to yourself in the Badlands."

I pulled it over my head, and just like that, the magic of my beautiful dress was gone. Only until I got to the castle. In my new dress, I could be whoever I wanted. Beta. Alpha. Royalty.

21

"Thank you," I said. Tavia didn't have to help. Even if she was my sister, all I had in the entire world, she could've reported me. If she did, I wouldn't live to see midnight.

"I love that you can still dream." She wrapped her arms around me. "One day, I hope I can again too."

THREE
ADALAI

The sun was falling quickly behind the horizon of the city borders and the party was in full swing. I sat, watching from my throne as several beta females danced to the boisterous music that filled the hall. They thrust their hips and swung their bodies so their gowns swished this way and that, revealing bits of lush flesh to catch the attention of hungry males nearby.

The seduction was working.

Alpha warriors whistled and eyed the betas as if they were a new prize to be won in battle. But what kind of prize was won by submission? When they threw themselves at a man instead of making him prove he was worthy.

It was fucking boring.

And I wasn't the only one who thought so.

At my right was Evander, dressed in the same formal attire as the rest of us, his face emotionless as a sheet of blank paper. To my left was Solen, fidgeting like he couldn't wait to be done with the formality so he could lock himself away and do his favorite thing... fuck. Even Cassian, who was naturally more good humored than the rest of us, looked annoyed as hell. The only one who was nowhere to be found was Dagger.

But the masses, it seemed, were enamored by the dancing females. So I let it continue.

I let my chalice dangle between my two middle fingers as I held it over the arm of the throne. Without a word, an omega servant refilled it with strong wine. Omegas weren't allowed in the city after dark but for special occasions such as battle celebrations, when they were needed beyond the hours allotted.

Bending rules was okay as long as you were king, and as long as they were of little significance. Slight curves instead of sharp angles.

So what if a few omegas had to find their way back to the Badlands by moonlight. It made them stronger didn't it, the struggles they endured because of The Division? That's what Dagger suggested. And besides, it wasn't fit for a royal to serve himself.

Scanning the crowd as I drank, I took in the array of color that gave the room an almost garish feel. Brilliant silken gowns of blue and green and purple. Roses of blood red, deep pink, and yellow like the sun. Sprinkled among all the bright hues was the gleaming black leather of the alpha males. The crowd moved like a multicolored wave and my gaze floated above it to the farthest entrance, counting down the minutes until I could walk through that archway and back to my quarters. The ancient books that lined my shelves were greater entertainment than this, even being written by men who lived in an America of times past.

A female appeared in the entry as if I'd conjured her out of thin air. One I didn't recognize. Not that I knew all the females of our pack. But she was definitely not one who frequented royal parties.

I measured her from across the dance floor.

Her gown would be called exquisite by the ladies. Her dark chestnut colored hair was braided into a crown around her head. She held her shoulders high, like she belonged here. Like she was born of royal blood instead of the more common blood of the betas.

But it was her eyes that held my attention when nothing else could. So wide and filled with wonder that I could see the blue of them even from a distance. Her face wasn't heavily made up like the other females in the room. Her decorations were faint, allowing me to take in her every expression.

Awe and surprise and hints of doubt that were quickly covered up by delight as her eyes danced around the room taking small sips of it all. Her gaze seemed to linger the longest on the roses. Did she like them?

I found myself wishing there were even more filling the hall just so I could watch her experience them longer.

Never taking my eyes off her, I leaned over to ask Evander, "The female who just entered. Who is she?"

"I am not familiar with her."

The tone of his answer had my attention snapping sideways to gauge his expression. He watched her just as I did, with interest.

A growl rumbled from my chest, not animalistic enough, not nearly. I wanted my beast now more than ever. My wolf would be out of my body so fast and at his throat—

"Stay away from her," I warned.

I watched his forehead fold up into a scowl as he turned to look at me. "Is that an order, my King?"

"Yes. And that goes for all of you," I told the

others just in case they wanted her too.

She was mine.

Mine until I grew bored with her.

And it would happen. Of course it would.

Because this existence was too empty to expect anything more. I lived to defend our people from the humans. To make sure they thrived and multiplied and grew strong. I lived to guide them into tomorrow, whatever it might hold. And then the next day, and the one after it.

Having someone by my side was never part of the deal.

Having someone soft to come home to was so far out of reach I couldn't even let the idea take root in my mind.

I swallowed hard as I watched the pretty female take a step into the crowd, her wide eyes constantly moving.

Until they landed on me. And she went utterly still.

As if she forgot to breathe.

Or was that my own lungs failing?

Her sapphire gaze clashed with mine for countless seconds before fluttering away. It fell to the floor like a cascade of autumn leaves and my heart picked up speed.

My mysterious beta was submissive.

But then her gaze lifted to mine once again, blatantly staring. As if she was deciding her next move. Measuring her next step using my reaction as a meter.

I stood, feeling more invincible than I ever did in battle. I had already captured her attention, now I was going to conquer her. I'd start with a dance. Ask as many questions as it took to learn her. And then take her to my bed and keep her as long as I wanted.

"More wine, my King?" the omega servant asked, pulling my attention away.

"No." I gave her my chalice and turned back to find my female.

But she was gone.

I scanned the crowd looking for her magenta dress, but she was nowhere to be found.

Where have you gone, female. Don't you know you can't hide from a king?

FOUR
ZELENE

I passed my first test, keeping my eyes averted as I went through the checkpoint on my way into Luxoria. The same guards traded shifts everyday, and they knew me. I didn't need to show the identification omegas had to keep on them at all times. That way, we could never be mistaken for someone we weren't. Someone who belonged in the royal city.

"Working the party tonight?" the guard asked. I made sure to get in the line of the one who smiled and told jokes almost every day. Not all of them were as kind as him. If I got in the wrong line, I might have blown my cover.

"Yes." Something like that.

"Be careful." He moved aside to let me pass. Only then did I notice all the guards held semi-automatic weapons. "The castle isn't always the safest place to be in the city."

I was a female omega. Nowhere was safe.

The other omegas working the party had been on shift for hours. Slipping in the service entrance, where I usually entered the castle, I made sure no one was around as I pulled my shapeless uniform dress over my head and hid it and my ID card on a pantry shelf, behind a bag of sugar. Pots and pans clanged in the distance, and I didn't have time to linger. I worked in the kitchen, and being here, dressed like this, was dangerous. My coworkers weren't necessarily my friends. They'd report me to save themselves from getting punished.

After twelve years working at the castle, I probably knew my way around the labyrinth of back hallways better than some of its inhabitants.

I had to move quickly. No Alpha or beta would have any reason to be in the kitchen, especially one considered a guest. Anyone invited to the castle only saw the absolute best the king had to offer, and the staff saw everything else.

I emerged from the shadows before I caught my breath. My heart raced as I entered the grand hallway, as if I only now realized what I'd actually done. The enormity of it. The consequences.

My beautiful dress had seemed so luxurious against the backdrop of dust and despair. Compared to the gowns that surrounded me, it was too short, too tight, and not enough to sell the story that I belonged here. Worse than that, the knee-length skirt showed the dirt on my feet. I hadn't thought about shoes until it was too late, and I wore the same tired slippers I wore every other day I came to this castle. Tavia helped me braid my hair. But I didn't have the flowing curls, the flowers, or the jeweled tiaras of the women around me.

I swallowed the lump in my dry throat. I'd die

in this dress tonight. But first, I'd experience a royal ball like I never had before.

A waiter I didn't recognize offered me a drink in a fluted glass. Maybe he wasn't omega. The castle brought people in to help with the big parties, for the important ones, they'd even hire betas. I'd watch him. Perhaps he was the answer to my problems.

I took a sip. Champagne. How long since I'd tasted the crisp drink? I had once risked a taste in the kitchens when no one was looking. Now, I could drink it freely. I indulged another long sip, savoring the sweet taste of liquid courage. I couldn't back out of my plan now, it was a surefire way to get caught. I had to own my faux beta status. If I didn't believe in myself, no one else would either.

I walked into the ballroom with my head held high, mimicking the actions of the royalty I served. They'd never be caught looking at their dirty feet, avoiding eye contact.

A band played in the corner, and couples

swirled around the room, dancing. Other groups had formed around the perimeter of the dance floor, and once again, I stood out. Everyone I knew at this party was getting paid a pittance to serve the revelers--that is, if they were lucky enough to get paid at all. Many weeks went by with nothing but excuses in exchange for our work, if they didn't find it satisfactory. As omegas, we had no recourse, and quitting was a death sentence. A bad reference from King Adalai himself would ensure no one else would take a chance on us. Tavia was living proof of that.

Again, I wondered what had caused her termination. But it didn't matter really. She was why I was willing to take this chance, to find a beta that would help me break the cycle. Then I'd be able to help my sister and our friends do the same. Somehow.

The wall near the window was lined with roses. Cool succulents accented the arrangement. Before The Division, my mother had lined our yard with blooms just like this. Back when our life had color and was full of hope. She was killed in the omega battles, on the front lines, doing whatever she could to give us a better life.

I couldn't let her down.

My eyes blurred at the memory, and I had to look away from the flowers. No one cried at royal galas, well, not in front of the guests, anyway. I'd shed more than my fair share of tears in the deep caverns of the kitchen.

Someone was looking at me. My wolf senses were at full attention. *No, please don't shift, not here...*

Omegas had one thing that no one invited to this castle had—the ability to shift into their animal form. It was our biggest and best-kept secret. No one from Luxoria knew we could access our animals. No one watched us close enough to know. We were pushed beyond the gates and forgotten until we were needed to serve.

If I sprouted fur here, in the king's ballroom, I'd be dead before I fully transformed.

I turned to look into the eyes of King Adalai.

He stared at me as though he planned to mark me.

Frozen in place, I didn't know what to do. I'd never been so close to him before. I worked in his house, helped prepare his meals, but we'd never been face to face. I couldn't look away, it would be disrespectful.

Or was it protocol not to look royalty directly in the eye? It wasn't something I ever had to worry about before.

The corner of his lips turned up in a smile that warmed my body from head to toe, and made the muscles between my legs pulse in time with my thundering heart. He was a beautiful man, with tawny skin and eyes that glittered, even from this distance. He rose to speak to a man dressed as richly as he was, in black leather pants and a matching jacket. This man wore a badge full of medals on his chest, so he was important too, but he didn't wear a crown.

There was only one king.

Dancers bumped into me, apologizing as what was left of my champagne rolled in my glass.

Both men were looking at me now. His Majesty said something else to the other man, and Rielle, my roommate, walked onto the stage with a fresh chalice full of wine for the King.

The men ignored her, but Rielle was one of the smartest women I'd ever met. We'd fought side by side for survival many nights, and there was no one I'd rather go to battle with. We didn't celebrate our victories so grandly in the Badlands, we just thanked the universe we lived to see another day. She looked into the crowd, her mouth gaping into an O when she spotted me.

Shit.

King Adalai turned to his friend once again, looking away from me, breaking the spell. My champagne glass shattered as it fell to my feet. The dirty slippers I'd tried so hard to not draw attention to would likely be streaked with blood when the broken glass hit my ankles.

Dancers gasped, and omegas were coming to clean my mess.

I had to get out of here.

Rielle would never tell His Majesty what I was, but I couldn't risk her slipping to another omega, or being questioned about her reaction. I hadn't thought this through. The pretty dress made me feel special, but it didn't change the fact I was so woefully unprepared to live in a world that didn't belong to me.

Guests were still arriving, and I bumped against them on the way out of the ballroom. I couldn't go out through the kitchen. Too risky. I wasn't as familiar with the castle on the grand level, where the royals loved to show off the riches and conduct business. I ducked into a side room, believing it would get me closer to the door.

Without my plain omega frock, I'd catch trouble as soon as I left the castle in this dress. No omega was allowed in city limits after dark. My dirty and bloody peasant slippers would give me away. My pale exposed legs. Even if the guards let me pass, the residents of the Badlands would make sure I never forgot my place again.

But the room wasn't an exit. Its walls were

made of glass, and the rest of it was drenched with color. An oriental rug, leather chairs, and flowers everywhere.

And there wasn't anyone else in it.

I sank into one of the chairs, giving myself a chance to catch my breath. To think of a way out of this mess. I looked down at my legs. Spilled champagne carved rivers in the dust on my shins. There was only one little nick from the broken glass, and the blood graciously had decided to stay near the base of the cut. The last thing I needed to do was bleed on this rug. The royals had technology that could track me with one drop of blood in seconds.

A door closed on the far end of the room. I pushed my body against the chair, not to be seen. My wolf was rumbling inside me, getting ready for a fight.

I smelled him before I saw him. A mix of whiskey, vanilla, and pure power. The King had found me.

What would a beta do? I smoothed my skirt

and sat straight in the chair. Proud. Like I belonged at a royal party.

He startled when he saw me. Only then did I notice the giant mahogany desk, and the even more impressive chair at the far end of the room. Had I walked into this office?

He could kill me for this offense, and no one would ever know, if His Majesty did his own dirty work. I prayed he didn't.

I kicked my shoes off, and used one foot to push them under the chair.

"You're bleeding." His voice was as soft as his jacket looked. I didn't expect that. Everyone knew of King Adalai's brutality. An omega like me, thought of it daily. But the tender way he sounded now only increased the strange pulsing in my body.

I nodded, hoping it disguised my trembling. The animal that was rumbling just below the surface of my skin. And that pulsing. I crossed my leg over the one with the cut to calm my inner muscles.

He frowned at my feet. There was no way he wouldn't see the dirt, or the telltale omega slippers that probably weren't hidden after all...

He's never been this close to an omega, my wolf said. *He doesn't understand what you are. You have a chance of getting out of this alive.*

I had to hope she was right.

"Some dancers bumped into me." Here I was, telling the king the same half truths that got me into this mess. "I dropped my glass. My shoes got ruined. I'm sorry."

"No need to apologize," he said. "But I don't understand why you weren't dancing too."

Clever royal. He'd just asked me who I was here with, thinking it would reveal who I was. My mind worked to whip up another of my half-truths in the hopes that when I pieced them together, they would somehow become whole.

"My girlfriends are dancing." I had no idea if this was how a beta was expected to speak to royalty. All I knew was that omegas never did. And there was the issue of eye contact. I risked everything and looked him in those beautiful onyx eyes. "I don't have a mate."

He laughed. My heart stopped beating as it plunged into my stomach. The only movement in the room was my pulsing muscles. This man had an effect on me. Maybe it was his power, the danger of being so close to him, but my body was going absolutely haywire.

"I don't have a mate either," he finally said. "But I'd like to dance with you."

Oh.

He held out his hand. It wasn't smooth as I might have expected. The king was a warrior who led his armies into battle against the humans. His hands were rough with callouses that would feel good moving along my skin. His nails were short and smooth with no signs of desert dust. He didn't wear any rings, but his leather cuff was held closed with a diamond link. My own hands were balled in my lap, clammy from fear, and ragged from years of hard work. If nothing else had given my status away, my hands would seal my fate.

Maybe he doesn't care. My wolf was begging to live on the wild side tonight. And no one denied the king.

I put my hand in his, and he brought it to his lips to kiss it. The soft contact jolted me.

The electric current that shot through my body was enough to make me shift. I squeezed my eyes closed, silently negotiating with my animal as His Majesty pulled me to my feet. His other hand was behind my back, pressing me against his body. Everything about the king was hard and ready for action. The heat that rose from his pants was enough to melt my skin. An image of the two of us naked, showered in moonlight, his lips all over my skin, flashed into my mind.

I took a deep breath, focusing on the roses beside us.

"You like those," he said. "I saw you admiring them earlier."

"They remind me of my mother." Finally, I could tell the truth.

"Mine loved them too. Now look at me, my

rose."

Now that I had his permission, I met his gaze boldly. He had yet to ask me my name, and I wondered what I'd tell him. If now that I was this close to him, I would ever lie again.

The truth was as deadly as not telling it.

Another image flashed before me, of the king in his wolf form. A form that had been ripped away from him. He was even more beautiful as an animal. I steeled myself, like I had to protect him from what was happening in my head. Hardly.

He stepped forward, just missing my bare toes, when the band started their next song. Shit. A beta would know these formal dances.

"You want to dance here?" That was a good save.

"Yes." The next step came from his hips, and pure instinct took over. I moved in time with his body. "Now that I've found you, I want to keep you all to myself."

Maybe it should have sounded like a threat, but to me and my pulsing body, it somehow sounded like... *a promise.*

FIVE
ADALAI

I didn't have to go far to find my female. Escaping through my office to avoid any unwarranted questions led me right to her. Except she'd been injured and was shaking like a leaf, and the instinct roaring in my chest demanded that I comfort her.

I didn't understand it. But I wasn't in the business of questioning my gut. Those instincts had led me down the right path too many times. In war. And pulling this woman close to calm her, definitely felt right.

"I haven't seen you around here before," I

murmured, not wanting to scare her. She seemed like she was seconds away from running again, even though I held her. There was a strength in her eyes. I could see it there, perhaps even her most admirable trait.

So then why did she seem like sand that could slip through my fingers?

"I don't attend these celebrations often, my King," she answered quietly.

"That's a shame." I swayed with her to the faint music that drifted through the walls from the ballroom. "I believe you're the exact delight all my celebrations have been missing."

"Delight." She laughed lightly, and still, she trembled even as her gaze remained steady. "No one has ever called me such before."

"A crime." Bending forward, I breathed in her scent. Sweet cinnamon and something earthy and unfamiliar. My unshiftable wolf stirred in my chest, loving the smell. "Shall I declare it punishable that a beauty like you isn't appreciated enough?" I asked. Reminding her of my power didn't seem like a terrible idea. Seemed necessary even. "Shall I demand that heads roll, my rose?"

She went stiff in my arms at that. "*No.*" Her voice came out strangled before she quickly cleared her throat and tried again. "No, it isn't necessary. Of course it isn't."

I pulled back, frowning down at her as she lowered her eyes once more.

Any other female would have laughed at the joke. Or at least blushed and swooned at my attempt at romance.

Fuck. I was no good at it. Never had been.

Usually didn't bother trying. But this time felt different. I wanted her to trust me.

"What is your name?" My voice was rough with desire. It was obvious, but I couldn't care.

She met my gaze again as her small tongue slipped out to wet her lips. "You first," she breathed, "Tell me something about you that no one else knows."

Her eyes were blue. Like sapphires. Looking

so deeply made me feel lost for several breaths. *Mine*, my wolf rumbled inside.

"I worry I will always be alone," I blurted. "That no female is strong enough to be mine, to walk beside me as a queen should. That this world is too twisted. Too fucked up for me to ever find someone to be one with, as my father before me did."

Shit.

I slammed my mouth shut. It was the only way to stop the waterfall of secrets from tumbling out.

The music faded.

We went still.

And my female stared at me with so much emotion in those cerulean eyes. Questions and fears of her own. And understanding.

Was she as alone as I was? Surrounded by others, but utterly isolated.

Our dance was finished.

"Your name." My breath chugged in my chest, every inhale causing her breasts to press against me. I swore I could feel the heat of her skin through the leather of my fine uniform.

"You are the king," she murmured instead, her palms flattening against my chest. "There is no reason you should be alone. You have servants at your call. People who adore you. Any beta in the city would be honored to be yours."

"None of them feel right. What's to be done about that?"

She cocked her head to the side, the corner of her luscious mouth twisting ever so faintly upward. "You should probably keep looking."

A new song started and she moved, forcing me to move.

A new dance. I'd take every advantage of it. Because I didn't want her out of my sight. Not now, after I'd stupidly allowed her pretty eyes to drag my innermost thoughts from my lips.

Maybe not ever.

I was the king. I could do that, keep her for as long as I wished.

But that wasn't what my chest was pounding

for. What had my throat dry and my palms sweating like a teenage boy who knew nothing of women or battle.

I wanted her to want what I wanted.

Which was what, exactly? Fuck.

A million betas could say yes to me tonight, and would, like she said. But only her yes would mean anything at all.

"Keep looking, huh?" I spun her carefully around my office, pretending the rug was our dance floor. "Just go through all the beta females one by one until there are no more. And then what? When I run out of betas and none of them are mine, what should I do then?"

The fantasy I had before, of mating with an omega female slammed into my mind, unwelcome and riling my animal even more. I blinked it away, but it grew into something new. A vision this time.

My nameless female beneath me, driving me mad with her scent. Her pheromones turning me into a crazed beast for her body. Her moans like music to my ears. Her claws raking down my back, begging me to ease her as I pounded away, desperate to fill her, to cool her heat.

In my arms, my rose shifted closer, pressing against my aching erection as we swayed. "Hm, running out of betas could be a problem. But I bet you'd find one you like first."

I eyed her. My wolf was trying to tell me something about her, but I couldn't grasp it.

"Maybe one I'd never seen before. One who won't tell me her name. Like you?"

She laughed, softly. Like she didn't do it often. "Me? Oh, I don't think you'd find what you're looking for with me either, my King."

"No?"

She pressed her lips together and gave a small shake of her head.

"What is it you suppose I'm looking for, exactly?"

"Well..." Did I imagine the way she stepped even closer? We were practically painted together now. She could feel my desire for her, pressing against her belly. "Let's see... you would need a beautiful female to be your queen. So beautiful that you'd never grow tired of waking next to her in the morning."

"Mmm." I let my thumb graze across the skin of her cheek. "One who blushes like a bloom under the morning sun." The pink of her cheeks spread all the way down her neck with my touch.

Her reaction gave me immense satisfaction.

"What else?"

She narrowed her gaze, studying me as if she could know what I wanted just by looking hard enough.

"A female who was worthy of you. One born into similar ranks."

I frowned at that, but she tipped her chin up, indicating she was such a female.

"What family are you from?"

"None that you know, my King."

"I know them all."

"Not mine."

"Were you born inside these gates?"

"Yes," she whispered.

My lips seemed to inch closer to hers with every word. I wanted to taste them. I would before the night was over.

"Tell me who you were born to."

Closer.

"Not yet."

Her hot breath mingled with mine, and still, I needed to get closer.

"What else?" I asked.

"You would want a female who does what you tell her."

"Only sometimes," I argued. "Like when we make love. I like to be in charge of fucking. I demand a lot, and I give a lot in return."

Her eyes went wide.

"Any other time, I want my woman to be bold." I tapped a finger softly at her temple. "I want her to challenge me, with questions." I moved my finger to her lips, tracing her mouth until she trembled with need. She wanted my kiss as much as I wanted hers. "I want her to tell me when I'm a pain in the ass."

"You're a pain in the ass," she blurted, and then slammed her mouth shut, eyes wide.

The expression on her face was so fucking adorable, I couldn't even be mad like she clearly expected me to be. Instead, my cheeks spread with a smile I couldn't keep back. When had anyone ever spoken to me so easily, anyone besides my men?

A chuckle rose in my chest as the music we danced to faded. In response, her smile grew too, until we both laughed freely. Hers sounded like morning bells announcing the sunrise.

Damn.

If anyone saw me now, like this, they'd wonder if I'd gone crazy. And maybe I had. But my rose made me feel...

Free.

Free, when I hadn't even known I was in chains.

She blinked, the teasing twinkle fading from her eyes until she looked... *sad*. "My name is—"

But I didn't want her feeling sad.

I didn't want the moment to end.

I wanted to forget about duty and my station, and be free a little longer.

So I kissed her.

My mouth crushed hers, too rough at first, but she didn't pull away. And when she gasped in surprise, I plunged my tongue inside to finally get the taste I'd been aching for. She was sweeter than honey. Hot and sultry, like summer used to be before everything beyond the walls turned to dust.

Her hands moved from my chest to around my neck, tentative at first but when our tongues tangled and danced, she grew bolder, winding her fingers through my hair to demand more. Asking things of me no one else had ever dared.

Easy answer: I'd give her fucking everything.

Feasting on her hot mouth, I backed her all the way up to my desk, her moans guiding me the whole way. Breaking the kiss, I pressed my lips across her jaw and down the column of her neck until I reached the delicious curves that were exposed at the top of her dress.

"I... my King... I..." Her words were breathy. She was losing her mind as fast as I was. "Something is... *happening*."

"Mmm, yes, my rose. Something is definitely happening." Her nails pricked my scalp as I kissed every inch of exposed skin. "You'll be mine tonight."

A helpless whimper left her throat. And gods, her scent. I couldn't get enough of that cinnamon earth. What was it? Why had I never smelled it before?

Her needy hands clamored at my leather, wanting skin. But she was either unfamiliar with undressing a male or too impassioned to work my clothing loose.

Either option was just fucking fine with me.

I released the clasp on my uniform and let it fall open. My rose pressed her palms to my chest, smoothing downward over the ridges of my stomach. Her touch was like flying to heaven, and I closed my eyes to savor it.

A soft growl rumbled from her, and my eyes came open to find her hungry expression staring down at my cock where it bulged the front of my pants.

Yes, female.

"You'll be mine tonight." *Forever*, my animal argued, but I ignored it.

I watched her eyes. Watched her pupils flare until they were almost all black.

"Mm, my King... I..." Her voice had changed. It was smooth and melodic with hints of desperation. She nearly writhed in my arms. "I need... I need *something*."

Her scent was growing stronger. I could smell her sweet arousal. She must be nearly dripping between those lithe legs.

"I have *everything* you need, female. Everything." I pulled her close to kiss her mouth again, this time gently, but she wouldn't have it. She nipped hard at my lips, growling as she pulled back, eyes wide with fear.

Fear?

Definitely fear.

"I have to go," she hissed, voice ragged. "I have to leave. Command me to."

I frowned. Command her to leave? When she was so needy, and I'd yet to pleasure her.

Never.

As if she hadn't just spoke, her lips pressed to my chest, kissing a path downward.

Yesss—

She pushed backward, putting space between us.

"I have to go, I have to go now," she whispered. "Right now. Leave, just *leave*." Was she talking to herself?

She whimpered as I tried to close the distance again.

Need.

Want.

Take.

Have.

Mine.

My wolf roared behind my sternum, and I was

nearly drunk with her scent.

She reached for me once again, but jerked her hand back before making contact.

What the hell was happening? What was wrong with my female?

Needs you. Needs you badly.

Then why was she moving so far away? Why was she inching closer to the door?

"My... *my* King," she almost whined, her face crinkling into a mask of despair. "I must go now. And you must let me."

I shook my head, feeling like I was in a great fog. Moving through jelly. Nothing was working anymore, least of all my wits.

I watched a single tear streak down her soft cheek, leaving a tiny trail of lighter skin beneath it. I knew what it meant, even if I couldn't bring myself to admit it yet.

Not yet.

I had to hold her. Keep her. Until I could think straight. Sort out what was happening with us.

But before I could reach her, she turned,

holding her stomach like she would be sick, and ran out of the office.

Ran away. Slipping through my fingers like desert sand.

SIX
ZELENE

This throbbing in my body, the crazed snarling of my inner wolf. I recognized what it was. I was in heat. A complication I hadn't seen coming. Now I had to get out of the castle before I seduced His Majesty.

Once again, I was running, this time barefoot with the taste of King Adalai searing my lips and this impossible pulsing between my legs. My muscles down there beat harder than my heart. Running was painful, especially since I didn't want to go back to the Badlands.

The King's body was hard in all the right

places, including the ones that said more than his words did. He wanted me.

He just smelled your heat, my wolf insisted. *And soon he'll realize you're omega.*

It was a death sentence. I'd played with fire, and swallowed the flame.

I ran smack into one of his men, his leather jacket a butter soft shock as we collided. Another complication. My scent could linger on that jacket, and one of them could figure out exactly what I was running from.

"Where are you going?" he asked, his low tone was undoubtedly a sexy invitation, but I shook my head as I untangled myself from his steadying grip. That pulsing would override every other function in my body soon, and I had to get some place where I was safe before I ripped off my pretty dress and begged the closest man, any man, many men, to take me. Hard and fast to match the throbbing.

I thought of the hard length of the king's erection that had been pressed against my belly just minutes before. His kind words, his deep voice vibrating over my body.

No.

I gripped my head in my hands, catching a flash of Rielle before I charged out of the grand ballroom. Again. She'd know what was happening, but she couldn't help me. My heat could trigger hers, and we'd both be dead before sunrise.

So I ran. Right out the front doors, like I'd been invited to come here. For a moment, I didn't know where I was. I always entered and exited the palace through the service entrance. The pebbles in the gravel stung my bare feet as I ran. Night had fallen on the city, and I hadn't gone back for my omega dress. I'd have to figure out a way to slip past the guards and get home unnoticed. Which on the best of days, was almost impossible. But with this pulsing taking over my entire body...

I had to focus. Nothing looked familiar. I always worked the day shift. I just needed to get to the Badlands as quickly as possible.

We had a system for masking our heat. There were old bomb shelters that had been built for the people who still lived inside the city to protect them from some long forgotten war. We used them to stay underground for the days it took our heat to pass. The male omegas couldn't scent us there. We were safe.

Right now, I was anything but. The pulsing became a flashing light in my vision and nausea rose.

I wasn't going to make it.

A narrow alley beckoned me, and I slipped into its darkness, and sank to the ground. Maybe I could stay here until the heat subsided.

My wolf had the nerve to chuckle. *Not unless you want to drive every man within city limits insane until they find the source of the scent and fuck it out of you.*

At least I could take a moment to get my shit together. Think about all the magical things that happened tonight before my body betrayed me.

I danced with King Adalai. He kissed me. And

it wasn't *just* a kiss. He claimed me. My skin tingled with the memory of his hard body pressed against mine, our tongues tangled, and his strong hands holding me close. Possessing me.

The pulsing between my legs intensified until I could barely see straight.

On hands and knees, I peered out of the alley into the street. The city was quiet. Anyone who mattered was in the castle, at the party, and those who didn't matter were already in the Badlands. Dizzy as I stood, I pulled down my dress, resisting the urge to rip it off, and wiped the gravel away from my knees.

My plan to get past the guards was enough to tamp down the urges, the impulses that came with the intensifying heat. I could offer to let a guard rut me, but there was no guarantee of my safe passage after I traded my body for that possibility.

Staying near the side of the road, I thanked the universe when all the guards were huddled together, laughing over something that probably wasn't funny. Their jokes were usually at the expense of the omegas.

The throbbing was like a double bass drum in my head, and it had to be echoing through the valley. But it didn't distract the guards.

Taking my opportunity, I ran.

"Hey!" A guard's voice echoed through the street. "That bitch is in heat!"

Oh shit.

My feet burned, ripped open from the old pavement that had fallen into disrepair. I knew the Badlands like I knew the service corridors of the castle. I slipped in between buildings, and hid behind the door of an abandoned storefront. Guards ran past, following the scent. I only had seconds to get to our shack, and I ran as fast as my broken feet could let me.

Crashing through the door, I woke up my sister, as well as Ashla and Charolet, our roommates.

"Zelene?" Tavia's concerned voice couldn't keep my attention as she rushed to help me. I was on the floor, finally able to give into the heat. My pretty pink dress was shredded and filthy as I tore it away from my body. "She needs to get to the shelter!"

Tavia held me in her arms, trying to soothe me. But I didn't want to be soothed. Not by her, and not like that. I wanted the king. I wanted that thick cock swelling inside me, spraying me with his seed. I wanted the royal heir growing in my womb.

Charolet brought over a bucket of cool water, splashing it on me. Transporting me to the shelter now was risky. My scent was too strong, and—

"The guards," I moaned. I'd been so glad to get home, safe for now, that I'd forgotten all about them for a moment. A luxury I couldn't afford. "They saw me."

"Shit." Charolet forced the word out between gritted teeth. "Where the hell were you, dressed like this?"

"She went to the victory celebration at the castle, thinking she could snag a beta," Tavia said with disgust. "I told her she'd get herself killed."

I meant to protest, but it came out as a feral whine.

Time moved like cool honey, thick and without definition. But eventually, the girls had me dressed in the only other frock I owned. Charolet wiped the cool cloth over my face before Tavia pulled me roughly to my feet.

There was chaos on the other side of the door. Each girl clung to me, pulling me back to the corner. But there wasn't any place to hide.

Someone banged on the door, nearly knocking it from the hinges. Another whine escaped my lips and there was no hiding that I was here. That was, if whoever was on the other side of the door couldn't smell my heat.

Any wolf's mouth would be watering, craving my juices. Whether he could shift or not.

"In the name of the King, open up!" An unfamiliar voice, but powerful nonetheless.

"If we live through this night, I'll kill you myself," Charolet muttered before letting go of me to answer the door. Every omega knew it was better to cooperate. The plan wasn't foolproof. But guards had carte blanche to punish us however they saw fit.

And once they realized I was a virgin…

Charolet gasped when she saw it was His Majesty who stood on the other side of the door. Still in his party clothes, the rich leather obscene against the backdrop of Badlands misery.

Guards stood behind him, guns drawn, pointed at my friend. Ready to kill first and ask questions never. But she didn't flinch.

King Adalai scanned the room until his dark eyes landed on me where I huddled in the corner. He went still, only moving to hold up my filthy slippers. "Forget these, my rose?"

SEVEN
ADALAI

I must go now. And you must let me.

Her last desperate words to me hammered through my skull with each step I took across the dry desert sand.

And she'd been right. My wolf watched her go, watched the space she took up in my office become empty as she got farther and farther away. The powerless beast had pawed at my chest to do something, even knowing that somehow, *some way*, I was bound by her words. King Alpha or not.

I must go now. And you must let me.

But she never said anything about hunting her.

I had found her slippers tucked under the chair in my office, confirming what my warring animal already knew.

Her shoes weren't the fine coverings of nobility. Not even those of a beta. They were broken and dusty. Rough canvas that served to barely protect the soles as one walked through the desert.

They were the shoes of an omega.

And she'd hidden them so I wouldn't know what she was while we danced.

Goddamnit.

My men tracked her scent to the gates of the city, but I didn't need their help finding her. That cinnamon smell was so deep in my lungs I'd probably never be free of it. My wolf was a constant growl in my chest.

Find mine.

Find and mark and mate.

No.

I wasn't traipsing out to the Badlands in the middle of the night to feel the moon on my back. I was going to find my rose and send her to the dungeons until I could figure out what to do with her.

I passed a row of shacks. They looked dark and brooding against the deep navy of the sky, slanting this way and that, none of them looking very sturdy.

When was the last time I'd bothered knowing the condition of the Badlands? Had I *ever* wondered about it or the omegas who called it home, aside from what they could offer us in service?

It never mattered how they lived before. Not really. This was their station. Just like mine was to rule from the luxury of a castle.

But it pummeled my mind now.

I shook off the feelings of guilt that shadowed me, and continued following the omega's scent.

It led me and my men to a shack at the edge of the desert. It was dark, as if empty. But the smell of omega heat was nearly overwhelming. One of the guards groaned, and I fisted my hands to keep from killing him. I wanted to kill them all. Each male that dared to breathe in the perfumed air. If they knew what was good for them, they'd fucking suffocate.

"She's in here," I growled at the same time my fist pounded the rickety door.

"In the name of the King, open up!" shouted one of my men as they pointed their weapons at the opening.

They could hurt the female, my wolf warned, as if it should matter.

Did it?

I couldn't explain my reaction, but the idea of my omega injured sent a wicked fire licking up my sternum. She must be kept safe.

Except before I could command my soldiers to lower their guns, the door creaked open and an unfamiliar omega stood in the dark hole it made. Beyond her, the dim moonlight illuminated my writhing female where she huddled in a corner with another woman.

"Forget these, my rose?" I rasped.

Her delicious scent wafted from the opening, polluting the air until I couldn't think straight. Rumbling with desire behind me were my men. They couldn't be here.

Get rid of them, the voice of my inner wolf snarled.

I stepped through the doorway, not considering my actions until I was too close. She was like a magnet drawing me. A siren, luring me to destruction. I stared down at her where she huddled on the floor. A needy sound escaped her lips and she inched closer to me, her shaking hand reaching out and nearly making contact before another omega jerked her back.

A growl left my throat. How dare they keep her from me.

"Please, Your Majesty. Forgive her," the closest omega stammered. "She's just come into her heat and doesn't remember she isn't supposed to touch an alpha. Let alone the king."

She thought I was angry because the female tried to touch me. Good. It was better they didn't know what had already happened between us at the castle.

Crouching low, I tried to meet my omega's gaze but she'd squeezed her eyes closed tight. As if... as if she was in pain. I didn't like the idea even though I should.

As if to confirm my suspicions, she grabbed her middle and moaned. "Please... Tav, help..."

"Shh. You have to stay calm." The other omega brushed her hair back from her face and blew as if to fan her off.

"Your Majesty..." The omega who opened the door came forward, her eyes lowered. "I understand that she has broken the law and must be punished. But if I might, I ask for mercy in this matter. Let us take her to the shelter until her heat has passed so that she might stand trial with all her wits about her."

"How long will her heat last?"

"Four days, about."

Four days of this torturous wanting. *Needing.* Would I be free of it when the heat was over? I didn't know.

My female moaned once more, scooting closer, her hand pressing forward again only to be smacked away by the omega who held her back.

"Never do that again," I snarled.

The omega's eyes went wide before lowering to the floor. "Yes, Your Majesty."

"Mmm, hurtsss." My female sawed her legs together, stirring up the dust on the floor.

"She's in pain."

"Yes, my Lord."

Good. She deserved the pain. Coming into my world, pretending to be something she wasn't. Making me want her the way I did—

No, my animal interrupted. *Help our omega. Soothe her.*

Shit. The command from my beast made me feel out of control. The urge to reach for her was so strong it took all my significant willpower to hold back.

79

"What can be done to help?" I asked the one holding my rose.

"Nothing, my Lord. Nothing except—" She stopped when another omega shook her head in warning.

"Except what?"

"Nothing except mating, my Lord."

Mating. My female whimpered at the mere word.

Mating.

My cock, which had been throbbing since the first taste of her lips, turned into a pillar of stone. I wanted to get inside my omega more than anything in the world. I wanted to obey my wolf and soothe her heat with my own.

The one who answered the door stepped even closer, causing my men to growl their warnings.

"But we're used to this," she said. "Know how to wait it out. How to…" She glanced nervously at my female. "How to survive. If you will only let us move her."

"Move her where?"

"To the shelter. Where we wait out our heats."

"Where is it?"

Her eyes went wide with surprise. "We don't disclose the location to males," she stammered. "It... it isn't safe."

"You will disclose it to me, female, and you will do it right now."

Her eyes flicked to a spot behind me and fear creased her expression. Turning to follow her attention, I noticed my guards coming closer—too close—their lusty gazes drilling into my moaning female. I could scent their arousal thick in the air, mixing with hers and it riled my wolf to the point I thought I could feel my claws pricking my fingertips.

But that was ridiculous. I couldn't shift.

Kill them. Kill any male who looks at mine. Who breathes her scent. Who lusts for her. Kill, kill, kill. Murderous thoughts clouded my mind, mixing with the fog of my female's heat.

I needed to get my rose somewhere safe,

away from any sniffing males before I went crazy and destroyed them all.

"Leave us!" I let the alpha note come through in my voice as I bellowed the command. The omegas flinched. Even the bold one who had opened the door. And my men finally snapped to attention, ducking their heads in deference. "Go. And don't come back to the Badlands for the next four days. It's my order that no one leave the city at all for the same span of time."

"Sir, there are omegas in the castle ."

"Where they will stay until I return. Understood?"

"Yes, Your Majesty."

"Go."

My guards turned and disappeared into the dusty darkness leaving me alone with the omegas. I found my female again. Her eyes leaked tears now, and it was impossible to describe what those tiny streaks down her face did to me on the inside. I felt ripped open but there was no rational reason for the effect she had on me.

Reaching forward, I caught a single drip with my thumb and smoothed it away. "How far to the shelter?"

I never took my eyes off my rose but I sensed the other omegas' confusion, felt them hesitate as they tried to comprehend what was happening, why the shifter king knelt on their dirty floor, worried about a hurting omega.

I wished them good luck figuring it out. Because I didn't understand it either. Maybe I never would. Maybe four days, and this feeling would leave me. I couldn't know. But I also couldn't walk away from her. Couldn't take her back to the city.

I was stuck.

She would pay for it. Somehow. But now, there was only one thing to do.

Carefully, I pulled her into my arms and stood. The contact with her body was like a million sparks of electricity shooting through my veins. But instead of paralyzing me, it was invigorating. Perhaps, I'd never felt this alive ever.

At least I couldn't remember any time that compared. My female's nails dug into the skin at the nape of my neck as she clung to me. As if she wanted to crawl inside me.

"Wait, wait!" The omega who'd held her stood too, looking panicked. "My king, please. What will you do with her?"

"You will show me where the shelter is. I will take her there."

The omega frowned, glancing to the other two in the small shack before meeting my stare again. "What do you intend to do to her?"

I lifted my chin. I didn't have answers. And besides, a king didn't have to explain himself. "Whatever I please, omega. Now show me the way."

"Yes, Your Majesty," the omega whispered, pushing past me toward the door.

"We'll all go," the stronger omega said.

"Just this one," I corrected nodding forward.

"You won't make it through the Badlands with her like this," she argued.

"I can protect her. And you will address me properly, female, or pay the consequences."

"Forgive me, my King," she squeezed through gritted teeth, "but it's true. She's too potent. Hounds will be on you before you reach the shelter, and you sent your guards away. You need us."

I knew the omega was right. My female's scent was strong enough to light up the entire midnight desert. There wouldn't be a male in the vicinity who wouldn't want to mount her. Just like my men had.

Shit.

These females were my only hope for getting her somewhere safe before it was too late.

"Very well. You can take the dagger from my boot for a weapon." I had another one at my waist and a third strapped to my back at all times.

The omega narrowed her eyes. "We don't need weapons. Come. Tavia will lead, Ashla will have your back, and I, your flank. We must hurry."

Out in the open air, the scent seemed to grow,

85

billowing out before us as we walked quickly and silently across the sand, passing quiet dwellings and closed businesses that were hardly more than shanties. The desolation of the place the omegas called home was glaring in the face of the grand war celebration I'd sat through earlier. I wondered how it felt for one like my rose to spend their days working in the city only to return to this dreary existence every night. To the drafty, dirty shacks to sleep.

The injustice of it nagged at me.

My father would have called it weakness. And it was. The omegas were segregated in The Division for a reason. A good goddamned reason.

Traitors.

Betrayers of the crown and shifter kind.

It was because of them we were hunted by the humans that remained on the continent. Because of them we were forced to close off our city and resort to the technology that kept us alive through the worst famines of modern times.

The betrayal of one group of omega defectors

had sent our way of life spiraling into something altogether new.

It was too long ago. I couldn't remember it. I only knew it took my mother from the world and left my father an angry vengeful beast. The Cold King he was known as, because he never ruled with his heart. Only his mind. Only with calculated strategy. He saw everything in black and white. Right or wrong. Never any room for gray.

The gray was pushed out of our city every night to wither away, punishment for the sins of generations past.

I stared down at the female in my arms. Her lips pressed tight into a line trying to hold back her whimpers. Her body throbbed, growing in frequency until she shook with the effort to refrain from crying out.

"Use my shoulder to muffle your sounds, female," I whispered.

She pushed her face into my jacket to let out a cry and her pain seemed to ease. Lowering my mouth to her temple, I pressed a kiss there. It was almost a thoughtless action. Natural. Instinctual. And she calmed even more.

"Thank... you... King."

The wind kicked up, sending the dust into a gray cloud around us.

Gray. No room for gray.

My father had taught me to see things the same way he did. No tolerance. No middle ground. But now, I'd seen *her*. A rose. Damaged and broken, but a rose nonetheless. Soft and sweet and giving me a reason to care. How was I supposed to go back to the way it was before?

An omega's heat lasted four days.

I just had to make it four days and things would return to normal. I had to believe it. This haze of need would be gone and I could be the king my people needed once again.

The omega beside me whispered, "We're almost there. Just over that rock base."

I followed the one called Tavia, counting down the steps until I was alone with my female. The wind was a measure of relief against her

88

overwhelming scent. Every dry gust, carried the earthy cinnamon that I wanted to devour away from me for precious seconds. Long enough for me to keep from laying her out on the sand and stripping her bare.

Almost there, almost there...

"We're being followed," the omega behind me murmured. Ashla was her name. She was quieter than the others but didn't hesitate to help get my female across the desert.

There was nothing in it for her. Not for any of them. But they left their shanty in the middle of the night to help get my rose to a safe place.

These omegas cared for each other. Like family. Or maybe they just had each other's backs because it was the only way to make it out here in the Badlands. Still, it was something the people of Luxoria didn't have. There was no supporting your brothers or sisters. No helping for the sake of helping. Only for *what* or *where* it could get you.

The omega beside me glanced over her shoulder, scanning the dark expanse of the desert.

89

"They've nearly caught up to us." She stopped walking. "Fuck. Scratch that. They *have* caught up with us."

Suddenly Ashla was in front of me, pressing her forearm to my female's face. "Lick me. Do it. Now, Zee."

My omega looked confused.

"What are you doing?" I demanded.

"It's the only way to dilute the scent. Spread it to us, and we'll lead them away. It will only work once she's underground, but if you hurry…"

"Lick, female," I growled down at mine. She frowned but obeyed, her tongue darting out to lap a trail up the omega's arm.

"More," Ashla said. The others had already crowded near. Tavia rubbed her hair all over my female, absorbing what she could from touch. "Your turn, Charolet. Hurry."

"Lick," I told my female again.

A wolf howled in the night, too close. But that was only partly what had the hair at my nape rising in warning.

A wolf. An actual wolf.

A wolf when there should be no wolves. Not in animal form anyway.

"They're here," Charolet hissed. "Coming up over the ridge. Get her underground. *Now*."

Tavia pushed me toward the rocks where the shelter was supposed to be. "Go. You'll see the opening under what looks like a piece of roofing tin. It locks from the inside." I charged forward but she stopped me with a hand on my sleeve. An action that could bring a death sentence with one word from my lips. "Please," she pleaded, "be kind to my sister. She's all I have in the world."

And with that, she turned back to the other omegas while I ran for the shelter, haunted by the feeling that everything I held in my arms was dangerous.

My female was dangerous. A ticking bomb ready to explode. Dangerous to my people, to herself. But most surprisingly, to my very own fucking heart.

***

The shelter was hardly more than a hole in the ground with a rickety ladder descending into the darkness. And fuck, we didn't have time for a ladder. Not with the wolf howling in the not so far off distance.

"Hold onto me tight, female. Tight as you can."

"Mmm." She groaned, her body undulating against mine as she wrapped both arms around my neck. Her lusty movements made me feel wild and her scent soaked into my brain, making it hard to concentrate. Made my wolf feel closer to breaking free than ever before. I could feel it pressing against my bones, wanting out.

Impossible.

Shaking, I climbed down the first two rungs, just enough to pull the hatch shut behind us and lock it. With the barest hint of moonlight, I could see the thick seal around the edges, looking out of place on the rough metal door. To keep the scent in. Smart. The omegas were smart.

Not wasting another second, I jumped into the unknown, bypassing the rest of the ladder and landing on my back with my female on top of me. Her audible *oof* from the impact was all I heard in the darkness. And even it somehow sounded sexy as hell.

Luckily, we'd landed on something soft instead of packed dirt or concrete. I blinked, letting my eyes adjust. It was pitch black inside the shelter, but my shifter abilities allowed me to see better than any human. In this moment, they seemed even sharper than normal. I could see the faint outline of the bedding we'd landed on, and beyond it, the dull functional walls of the shelter.

My omega's eyes glowed above me as our gazes clashed.

"King," she whispered, her warm breath making me feel dizzy with desire.

"Tell me your name, female." I needed to know it. Needed it on my lips. Needed to say it over and over until it was as natural as breathing.

"I'm Zelene." Her voice shook with fear so strong it was palpable, but her body moved on its own, legs straddling my waist, thighs squeezing against my hips. Hot center grinding against my cock. "Will... you... kill me for what I've done?"

"I don't know."

"I..." A strangled needy sound rose up her throat. "... didn't mean for this to happen."

I surged up, flipping her onto her back. I was alpha. Not meant to be under an omega. I was powerful, I was king. And I intended to show her every bit of that power by the time we left this place.

"Didn't mean to," I purred, loving the way her chest lifted and fell with each of her labored breaths. It hypnotized me. "Didn't you dress pretty and come into my castle as a beta instead of a servant?"

"Yes."

My hand grazed the fine skin of her jaw, helpless to keep from feeling her now.

"Didn't you dance with me as if you deserved to?"

"Y-yes."

Shame filled her expression, mixing with the

94

lust and fear. My cock considered it a winning combination.

"Didn't you steal my breath with your smile?"

"Yes?" She frowned and my thumb smoothed along her lower lip, remembering the feel of her mouth.

"Didn't you kiss me with those sweet fucking lips?"

"No."

I narrowed my gaze in challenge. "No?"

"*You* kissed *me*," she whispered.

Her boldness shocked me, though it shouldn't have after the stunt she pulled. She kissed me back. She had let me taste her. I wasn't letting her deny it now. Not here, when we were finally alone and no one could judge us.

"Didn't you want me to?"

"You're impossible to deny right now, with my heat battering away at me."

"You weren't under your heat when we kissed. Don't pretend you didn't want me, omega."

"But I am in heat now," she argued, her voice

trembling.

"And you want me even more."

She shook her head, eyes going wet as she bit hard on her lip, pulling it away from my thumb. "Not want. *Need.*"

"Want," I insisted.

I knew the difference. I wanted her the first time I saw her in the ballroom. I needed her when I scented her heat. The two feelings mixed together, twisting into something that had its own name. But I wasn't ready to think about that yet.

I dragged my fingertips down her throat to the edge of her collar, feeling her hard swallow beneath my touch. "I won't touch you because of *need*, woman. Not even to ease my own." She had to want it as much as I did.

"It hurts," she breathed.

"I know. Tell me the truth. You *want* a king. You want to be the omega who brought the shifter king to his knees in a dirty Badlands shelter."

"No!"

"You want a king's cock between these legs,"

I said softly.

"No," she snapped, choking on a sob as her body tensed in another painful contraction that pushed her hips into my rigid erection. "I just want you to look at me like you did in the royal office. Like I'm beautiful and desired and... and *worthy*. And if my heat hadn't started, maybe I could have pretended I was someone else in a king's arms for just a little while longer. Because trust me, that single dance was the highlight of my fucking life." Her words came rushing forward as if her body needed to expel them to relieve the pressure. "But that's not how things happened, and I tried to leave. I tried. But you followed. So if you aren't going to touch me, if this is your way of torturing me before you have your soldiers end me... then... then just *leave*. Leave and let me suffer through this alone."

There she was. There was the female I recognized from the ballroom. The one who had fooled me into thinking she was more. *Mine*. My wolf repeated the claim again and again inside my

97

mind.

Sweet, stubborn omega.

She didn't mean to, but she'd just given me all the information I needed.

I eyed her in the darkness, gaze digging in to reach the parts of herself she didn't want me to see.

"You. Want. Me."

"I want you," she choked out.

Her eyes were pained and somehow, I knew it wasn't only physical. My female had a ragged heart that needed attention. It had been beating through the cuts and bruises life had given her. Maybe even I had given her without understanding.

Instinct demanded I soothe her. And for the next four days that was what I intended to do. Consequences be damned.

"Prove it," I demanded.

"How?"

"Kiss me."

Vibrating with repressed need, she eased

forward to meet my lips, but I stopped her.

"Wait."

She went still, waiting for my command.

"Kiss me as if there were no alphas and omegas, and nothing in between. As if there was no king, and we were just a man and a woman finding each other for the first time, no future to worry about except the one we could create. Kiss me... like a rose. *My* rose."

She stared at me, blinking, while I held my breath to see what she'd do. *Do it, female. Show me what you're made of.*

With a desperate sound, she surged up, her mouth slamming down on mine in a hard kiss before her tongue forced its way in to tangle with my greedy one. I didn't want to leave any corner of her mouth unexplored. She tasted like sin and silk. Forbidden and so, so smooth.

Mine.

I found her hand, bringing it over her head to keep it from wandering. I needed to keep control, and I was so damn close to losing it. My mind, my station, my senses.

My humanity.

My insistent inner animal was pushing me to the edge of breaking. What would happen if I gave it full control?

Zelene sucked on my lip, pulling it between hers and earning my growl of approval. But to my surprise, in the next breath, she bit it hard enough that I tasted blood.

"*Fuck*." I jerked back, staring down at her. Her eyes glittered with challenge.

"How's that for proof?"

Like all roses, mine had thorns.

Grabbing the collar of her thin dress in both hands, I jerked hard, ripping it clean down the center to reveal her small breasts. The tips were swollen and proud, and my mouth watered for a taste.

I dove for one, lashing it with my tongue once, twice before pulling it between my lips to suck and toy with.

My rose cried out at the contact, half-pain,

half-pleasure, and her fingers threaded in my hair to keep my head where she needed it.

"More, *more*," she begged.

I moved to lave her other nipple before winding a trail down her ribs, kissing and licking the scent from her soft skin, swallowing it down like medicine for my soul. Fuck. When her legs were spread wide and her wet sex inches from my mouth, I couldn't go slow anymore.

I dove for her throbbing center, licking up her juices and sucking her clit between my lips. Her taste was better than honey. As her hips writhed against my mouth, I pushed my tongue deep into her, desperate to drink her down, her moans urging me on. I fucked her with my mouth until her body tensed tighter than a fist, and she let out a scream as pleasure ricocheted through her.

I jerked back, rising to my knees above her. She needed my cock. Needed it now.

Sliding a finger between her wet folds, I found that tight pulsing hole and pressed inside, testing her. But to my shock, I hit the tell-tale barrier that told me she was…

"Fuck," I snarled, sucking in a hard breath to get my bearings.

Take her. Take her now, my wolf demanded.

I wanted to slam into her hard. Bust through that barrier in a way that made her irrevocably mine. I was King *fucking* Alpha. It was damn near my right. If I want it, I take it. And I wanted Zelene more than anything.

But…

I wanted her to *give it to me*.

"King?"

I sucked air, trying to keep steady, and pressed my palm against her throat.

She was a virgin. My female was untouched by any man before me. The satisfaction that brought me was like nothing I'd ever experienced. Not in battle, not in my bed. Not even with that first kiss we shared in my office.

My wolf told me she was mine. This just proved it.

"Tell me what you want."

I felt her swallow against my hand. The action was one of trust.

"You," she whispered. "Just you. Right now."

"Are you sure," I asked her. I would only ask once. She was only getting one chance to change her mind about this.

"I'm sure."

Relief swept over me like a wave. She shouldn't trust me. Especially not this much. But she did, and it made the alpha in me want to beat his chest.

"Are you?" she gasped when I released her throat. "I'm fertile..." The words faded out on a whimper that sounded so much like the animal she housed within. "You know what this means, king." Her legs sawed desperately around my hips.

Was I sure?

It was forbidden. So fucking forbidden. I could lose my crown for this. I could lose everything.

The heat from her core burned my cock. I

needed to bury it in her, fast and hard and firm. I needed to stay there until my knot swelled with seed, and she milked it from me. Brand her with it like she branded me.

Forbidden, forbidden...

But instinct raged within me.

Worth it. She would be so fucking worth it.

With a roar, I surged forward, spearing her center to take what she was so ready to give.

There was no going back now. King or not, forbidden or not...

The omega was mine.

EIGHT
ZELENE

Tonight, the king was supposed to be celebrating victory. But right now, he belonged to me.

The power of that knowledge mixed with my heat made me high as he thrust inside me. Hard and fast and mad with need. This is what I'd craved, month after month as I sat down here alone in the dark, writhing in the filth, dreaming that someone would come and take the need away from me. I'd never given myself the luxury to think about want, as His Majesty demanded I do. He was used to putting himself before everyone else. For me, that was a death sentence.

But as I curled my fingernails into the leather of the king's jacket and took his lips as mine, I let myself dream. That this was more than my heat turning him into an animal. That a man like King Adalai could see me as something more than an omega. More than a female body to rut whenever he pleased. He'd given me a taste of something dangerous. Want was becoming hope.

I didn't only want to belong to the king. I wanted the king to belong to me. Like he said, I wanted to be the omega who brought the shifter king to his knees. Not only in this filthy bunker, but in front of the entire city.

My dreams and my pride would get me killed, so I would hang onto this night fiercely. The king could end me tomorrow. Tonight even. He could throw me to the guards and let them have their way with me until I couldn't take anymore.

The king pulled away from my mouth. His cock still throbbed inside me. We were one.

"What's the matter, my rose?"

"Nothing," I lied.

I could barely make out his features in the dark, but there was no missing his frown. Was it possible that the king actually cared about me?

I had to keep my wits about me. He never promised not to kill me.

"Is it not how you expected it to be for your first time?"

"No." I had the nerve to laugh, feeling drunk on the sensations he pulled from me. Rielle had smuggled some ancient romance novels out of the castle library and we all had a good chuckle while she read them out loud. But when she was done, all my housemates were left with that same wistful expression. Maybe it could be like that, and not hard and rough like some omegas were forced to serve the guards. The unlucky ones who didn't make it to shelter in time.

"Then what did you expect?" These words weren't as kind.

"It's better." Yes, he was hard and rough and he meant to claim every inch of me and remind me

107

beyond the shadow of a doubt that I was omega and he was King, but the king *wanted* me. He'd tracked me down. He could've had any female within the city walls. He wanted me. "Because I'm with you."

He sighed, rolling back onto his knees. His cock was no longer inside me, and the pulsing had become instant insanity in his absence. Buttons popped against my skin as he pulled his jacket open, revealing his hard, muscled chest. The leather slid down his arms, to the mattress. He was so beautiful, so real in his vulnerability. So mine.

For now.

An involuntary whine escaped my lips. Day one of the heat wasn't even the worst. It crested in violent waves, and I had no idea how long the King planned to stay. Planned to let me live.

I reached for his cock. I needed it inside me, in any way possible. His big hand closed over mine before I had a chance to lean forward and close my mouth on it.

"I control the fucking, female." His tone was terse. But he didn't take my hand away from his shaft.

"I need it," I groaned between clenched teeth. Through my mania, I remembered our conversation from just moments before we started rutting. "I want it. Please."

The King ran his other hand over my dampened hair, smoothing it away from my face. "You want to suck my cock?"

"I do. I want to take you as deep as I can." My head was swimming with my heat. I had no idea if I could make good on my promises. I'd never put a man's penis in my mouth before. But now the opportunity was here, and I had to do everything in my power to convince his majesty not to kill me.

It wasn't why I was doing it. I needed him inside me. But I was terrified I couldn't satisfy the king the same way he could satisfy me.

A moan escaped from his lips. "That's a good thing, my rose. Because I would like to fuck your mouth."

His grip tightened on my hair and he guided his cock to me. Once the tip hit my lips, he let go of it, easing it along my tongue and hitting the back of my throat. I startled, but he adjusted his rhythm.

"Drop your hands, Zelene." My name rolling rough and ready off his lips sent a shiver down my spine.

I did as I was told, letting him guide his hardness between my lips. I barely had a chance to catch my breath, but I loved it. His Majesty, for all his stern words, wouldn't hurt me. While we were together, I could let myself believe this fantasy. I'd carry it with me as long as I could through my heat.

"Touch yourself," he commanded.

My arms had gone to rubber, and I covered my breasts moaning against his cock as my fingers moved over my pebbled nipples. They ached for this.

"That's good." His voice was more like a purr

now. "But I want you to go lower. Touch your clit for me, my rose."

I did as I was told, pushing the bunched-up ruins of my dress from my stomach down to my thighs. A zap of electricity flooded my body on contact, and I rubbed in time with His Majesty's thrusts. My body writhed, the heat taking over absolutely everything. I thought I would melt into a puddle of need and desire in this bunker, on my knees before the king.

The pressure continued to build and my head fell back as I cried out. I came, my juices soaking my fingers. I was losing control of everything, but I couldn't stop. I was addicted to this feeling. Forcing my eyes open, I wanted to see the King. He was more beautiful, more powerful than ever, in a climax of his own. Ribbons of his seed landed on my chest.

I lay panting on the mattress as I came down from my orgasm. My hand was still between my legs, the heat and the throbbing had yet to subside. His majesty frowned slightly, running his fingers through the ribbons of cum on my body and offering it to me. I drank it down, sweet and salty, sad that he wasn't inside my pussy when it happened. I couldn't birth his heir.

This time, I thought as I drifted into blackness.

***

The worst part of my heat was the fever dreams. They were so real, and I couldn't stop them because it was impossible to wake from them until they were damn good and ready to be over. Tonight, I dreamed of the king in battle. It was an old-fashioned fight, on horses with suits of armor and bows and arrows. A bloody, hand to hand fight where a warrior could look his opponent in the eye and watch him take his last breath. I gasped awake just before Adalai's enemy sank a knife in his armor.

We weren't safe. We may never be. Would he invite me to fight by his side, or would I be that opponent, eye to eye in battle?

My heart pounded as I tore myself away from

the dream. Blinking, I let my eyes adjust to the new darkness. The second day of my heat. My body throbbed, which was nothing new, but now, there was an unfamiliar ache that lived in the center of my chest. A pain of missing His Majesty.

I assumed he was gone, back at the castle with his men. It was a lost cause, but I hoped he didn't regret what we'd done. I was still alive, that had to mean something. Safe in the bunker. More lucid than usual on day two, but I knew it was only a brief reprieve.

A slight breathy hitch alerted me that I wasn't alone.

The room still smelled like sex. An unbroken heat had a completely different scent. And now I knew a heat didn't exactly break. I'd hoped that being with the king would make these horrible symptoms go away. The pulsing between my legs had lessened, replaced with a dull ache.

I turned my head, expecting to see one of the girls—our heats synchronized like clockwork. Tavia, as my sister, usually turned within days of me, but it wasn't her. It wasn't any of the omegas.

Asleep on the bed beside me was King Adalai.

He had stayed. The king actually stayed.

I blinked away the unexpected wetness in my eyes.

His soft snore brought a smile to my lips. He might be royalty, but he was so much like me. Like us.

In that moment, I knew we were the same. The same hearts, the same oxygen in our lungs. I put my hand lightly on his heart just to feel it beat.

Bad idea.

In a flash, he grasped my arm, bending it back from my body as he pinned me to the mattress with his hips. Pressing my lips together hard to keep the scream inside, I shuddered underneath the weight of his body when I saw the look in his eyes. It was the same one from my dream, when he was on the battlefield, just before he killed.

"I'm sorry," I finally forced out, when I thought I'd die from the intensity of his stare.

"Never do that." He dropped a quick kiss to

my forehead and rolled off me with a sigh. "Good morning."

Good morning?

"Hi." The fear rushed out of my body, replaced with curiosity. "How did you sleep?"

He ran his hand down his chest muttering, "Better than I have in ages."

"Good."

He turned to look at me. "Is it? Good? What if I wanted to punish you for this stunt. How am I to do that when you have this effect on me?"

"Will you punish me?"

"I haven't decided yet."

I propped my head in my hand, unable to contain my grin as I raked my gaze over him. Rumpled from sleep, for once he was less than perfect. Less than kingly. He was *normal*. And my poor heart, which had been getting quite the workout ever since I came up with this crazy scheme, skipped a beat. This secret moment with him meant too much.

I was falling for King Adalai. His name would

be on my lips when he killed me for this.

"I'm glad you stayed," I said, filling the thick silence.

"I couldn't leave you alone down here. No guards—"

I laughed. "You think I usually have guards? Because that never happens. The best I can hope for is one of the girls to be in heat at the same time as me. You mean *you* didn't have guards to take you back to the city."

It would've been dangerous for the King to walk through the Badlands without protection. And he was well within his rights to kill me for pointing it out. There were plenty of omega males with a chip on their shoulder who would love the bragging rights for taking down His Majesty.

"I don't need anyone's help, female." He slammed his hand against the mattress. "I stayed because I wanted to make sure you made it through your heat safely."

Stars exploded in my vision. King Adalai just admitted he cared about me.

"Thank you, Your Majesty." But something about this man pushed me to test every single boundary. "Does that mean you want to fuck me again?"

"You have a smart mouth for an omega."

The pulsing between my legs was back. Needing him. Wanting him. "Does that mean you'll punish me?"

"You keep asking like you want it to happen, my rose." He turned to face me. Mirroring my position, with his head propped in his hand. "I could bring you to the public square and take my sword to you in front of the entire city." He ran his hand from my mound all the way up to my throat, clasping it into his grip. "They'd cheer as you begged for your life."

"But would you?" I asked. "And if I begged for my life, would you let me live?"

He didn't say anything right away. "Brave. Sometimes it's the same thing as stupid. But it's also the only way to win a battle."

I closed my eyes for a long blink. In the wake

of this crazy dream, that I could get a man who lived inside the city walls to treat me like one of his own, so many more had blossomed. I never dared set my sights on the King, but here we were, in the heat bunker, tangled in sex-stained sheets, together. I was teasing him and I could actually see his walls crumble. Maybe I could show him my people weren't lesser than his. We were all the same.

Or maybe he was right. Bravery and stupidity were the very same things.

"You can go back to the city if you want. It's probably daylight. One of the girls will come check on me." We always took turns, making sure whoever was in heat had food and water, even if they weren't in any shape to consume it. Coaxing them to eat and drink, we'd stay as long as needed.

"Your friends care about you very much," he said.

"They're amazing women. I know you probably don't think of them that way, because we're omega, but we do the best we can with whatever we have." I almost told him why I'd come to the party, because I truly believed we only needed one alpha or beta to see that, to see *us*, and it could change everything, but I was already pushing my luck, and my body could betray me at any moment and go back to a state of pure need.

"I was impressed with how they came together to protect you last night. They put their lives on the line to make sure you were safe."

I nodded. "That's how my mom taught us. Tavia's my sister, and the other girls were orphaned early in the war, so Mom took them in, and we've been together ever since."

"Where's your mom now?" he asked.

I swallowed hard. "She died in an Omega War battle, trying to keep the Badlands a part of Luxoria." It was still hard to talk about my mom. She'd been gone ten years, but every day I saw something that reminded me of her around our shack. Even the way Tavia talked. I always teased her about it, but I loved it just the same.

"I'm sorry," the king said softly.

I was thankful for the dark, so he wouldn't see my tears. Mom taught us never to show weakness. Not even when our backs were against the wall. "Me too. Mom taught us how to fight, to question everything, and not to take any shit from anyone inside the city."

I probably said too much. Maybe he would want to know who she'd been aligned with, and ask if the omegas had any secrets. We only had one. Our ability to shift. But our energy went into surviving. Didn't leave a lot of time to overthrow a government.

"I like her." The King wiped the tears from my cheeks. To make sure his work was complete, he sealed it with a kiss.

I kept asking him, teasing him, if he'd punish me. But this time, I was too scared to ask. My mother would've served us his father's head on a plate for dinner and topped it with mashed potatoes, since we only got those on special occasions. Up until now, I was just a clueless omega who'd overstepped her bounds and managed to lure the king into the Badlands by the promise of her virginity. He had it, and he hadn't left. Now he knew everything about me. Too much.

"What happens now?" I asked, my voice barely a whisper.

"Are you still in heat?"

I nodded. "I will be for three more days. It's...more manageable than usual after last night. I think, anyway. I can speak in complete sentences and I don't feel like my wolf is trying to tear my skin open. But..."

Apparently, sex had been like a truth serum and I didn't know when to shut the hell up this morning. If my actions didn't get me killed, my words would most certainly be the end of me.

"But what, my rose?" And the King, I wished I could think of him as Adalai now, even if I couldn't address him that way, was being so nice. It scared me more than when he was formal with me.

"I don't know how long the effects will last." I stretched to give my animal some room as she squirmed inside me, and a whine slipped out.

Shit.

I wanted him to think I had control over my body. That I could be just like him.

"Have you ever shifted?" he asked.

"No." The pressure was building again, especially with the scent of our union still heavy in the air. With my naked body next to his. But he had to be testing me, to see how much I was willing to give him in exchange for my life. How far I was willing to go. "We can't shift either."

Which was the biggest lie I'd told since I entered the castle in my pretty pink dress. Last night already seemed like a lifetime ago. The wolves had been circling the bunker all night long, howling with need but unable to find the source of the scent. The King must have heard them too. I'd been more than a little preoccupied, but they did it every time a female omega came to ride out her heat.

"What would you do if you could shift?" he asked, pushing the issue just that little bit more.

I closed my eyes. A wave of heat and need came over me. "I'd run free. There wouldn't be any alphas or omegas. We'd all be wolves."

"But wolves have packs, and packs have leaders," he reminded me.

"And every wolf has something to offer the pack. No one is lesser or more than another. One is just the leader." I writhed beside my King.

"Omegas have something to offer." It was big of him to admit that. "They keep our city running while we keep it safe."

"But you don't keep us safe." I couldn't take it anymore. I pushed his chest down onto the mattress and straddled him. The moan that escaped his lips was so satisfying. But every move I made, every word that came out of my mouth, got me deeper into a place I wouldn't be able to dig myself out of. "Do you know how many omegas have gone missing over the past few years?"

"Missing?" His frown told me he was oblivious to the strange abductions none of us could explain.

"You've seen how we live. My friends and I watch each other's backs because we have to. Or the—"

My head fell back and I let out a whine before I had a chance to say *the wolves would get us.* They'd bring us to their very own bunkers and have their way with us. Just like I was hoping the King would do with me. Everyone suspected it was omega on omega violence contributing to the missing persons, but it wasn't just females missing.

His Majesty grabbed me by the throat, and before I knew it, I was the one with my back on the mattress, with his hot thighs caging me in.

"My little omega wants to know what it would feel like if she lived in my castle," he whispered, then nipped my ear. "You don't just want me on my knees before you. You want the entire city to kneel for you."

"No." I was panting, half-mad with need. "I just want you inside me."

He reached between my legs, and when he revealed his fingers, they glistened with my arousal, even in the low light. "Don't lie to me, Zelene. Are you satisfied, living like this, wondering if you and your friends will live to see another day?"

He knew I wasn't.

"You can do something about that." I swiveled my hips, grinding against his hard cock. "You make the rules. You can change them."

Sweat poured out of my skin. My legs were wide open, an invitation for the king to impale me. My heat pounded, and my animal was so restless just below the surface.

He frowned. "It's not that easy. Nothing ever is."

"You're the king." It was getting harder to talk, and he knew it.

"That's right. I am." With one smooth thrust, he slid his cock inside me. The relief was almost instant as he rocked his hips back and forth, his balls slapping against my sensitive lips. I cried out, trying to tell him I wanted more, how good it made me feel, and about the sweet, sweet relief he gave me, but I was beyond words now. He kept one hand on my throat. The other pinched my nipple, and he nodded with satisfaction as I whined.

The intensity grew with each thrust. His shaft swelled inside me, bulging until his knot was tight against my opening, locked into place, and he groaned as his balls hitched.

I gasped at the first hit of hot spray, coating my inner walls. They pulsed wildly, milking his shaft for more, more, more. The heat was unbearable as I lost all control, crying out in unison with the king.

We stayed locked together until he drained. I felt a little sad as his knot subsided and he pulled out of me.

He had yet to catch his breath, sitting with his head in his hands.

I pulled myself up to a sitting position and dared to put my head on his shoulder. Usually, this was the line he would not let me cross, when we went from omega and alpha to something we couldn't define. But this time, he didn't push me away.

He put his arm around me, tucking me close, and shook out, "What have I done?"

NINE
ADALAI

I'd given her my seed. An omega who was fertile and ready to grow with my child inside her. I knew what I was doing, and did it anyway. Why?

Not because I was out of my mind with lust, though I had been. Wanting to knot her to completion like nothing else in this world.

Not because I had forgotten who I was or who she was, though the line between us was blurring to nonexistence.

No, I had emptied myself deep inside Zelene because I wanted to claim her as mine. No one had ever called to me the way this omega did. No one made me wish I was someone else just so I could have her. And it wasn't only the heat making me feel this way. I'd known she was mine the moment I first spotted her in the ballroom.

I held Zelene in the dark, my fingers digging into her flesh. And I knew it was too hard, but the animal inside me was desperate to keep her.

Keep her.

That's what I intended to do wasn't it? I didn't know how, but it was my priority now.

You make the rules. You can change them. She'd said those words and she believed them. As if I could just snap my fingers and change the omega laws. As if I could abolish The Division altogether. But it wasn't so simple. Leading never was.

I pressed a hard kiss to her forehead and stood, making my way through the darkness to the sink that sat against one wall. My hand shook as I twisted the faucet to hot. A small shelf above it held a stack of folded cloths. Pulling one down, I wet it under the warm stream before returning to the bed.

"Lie back."

Zelene frowned but scooted backward. "What are you doing?"

"Shh. Just obey me, omega." My voice barely worked, but she listened, and I crawled up the mattress until I was on my knees before her.

On my knees truly, for the first time.

Somehow, I knew it wouldn't be the last.

Starting with her forehead, I ran the cloth over her skin, washing away the dust and sweat.

"What are you doing?" She whispered the question again.

"Taking care of you."

I dragged the warm cloth down her neck and over her shoulders.

"There's no need." Her voice was so soft. Like I'd shocked her. Touched her. Affected her. Good. "I'm fine, my King."

King. I didn't want her calling me that anymore. We were past formalities. I was willing to die for her. She could damn well call me by my name.

"I'm not your king." I glanced up to see her frown. "I'm more than that now."

She swallowed hard as I smoothed the cloth across her tits, nipples perking in reaction.

"What should I call you then?" A whimper escaped her throat as I did a second pass over her sensitive nipples just to torture her. "Judge? Executioner?"

She was still worried I'd punish her, when the mere idea of causing her harm sickened me.

"Defender," I corrected, "but Adalai is fine."

Zelene went stiff beneath my hands and I stopped washing to find her scowling at me through the dark. "Defender?" she croaked.

What was it about that word that petrified her?

"Defender," she tried again. "Are you being cruel?"

"*Cruel*," I scoffed. "By offering my protection?"

Quick as a blink, she slipped out of the bed and began pacing the small bunker. "Why would you offer me protection? Protection when you should be punishing me," she muttered, almost to herself. "It doesn't make sense."

"Come back to bed," I ordered. "You need to be cleaned. And we need food."

Her gaze snapped to me. "Food? You won't find any here."

I frowned. "The omegas would refuse their king away from his castle."

"No. Not refuse you." She resumed pacing. "They would likely give you their last crumb for fear of being punished if they don't. But that's all you would get. A crumb. Because out here, no one brings us meat on a platter or bread with sweet butter in a tiny pot on the side or wine in fancy goblets. Out here, we are *starving*."

Her words were like a punch in the gut. It was like I was just now opening my eyes to all the injustices a third of our shifter population endured. How could I have been so blind? One night I went to bed believing the omegas deserved their lot. And after twenty-four hours with Zelene,

133

I was convinced the royals—specifically, I—was the villain in her story.

The wolf inside me wouldn't stand for this. *I* wouldn't stand for this.

"You've suffered too much, my rose. I won't let it continue. I promise you this."

Her eyes went wide as she shook her head. "No, no, no. You're not supposed to care. You're the king. The one who enforces the laws that keep omegas set apart. The laws that keep us confined to this dried up desert."

She was clearly upset, but hell if I knew why. Because I realized things within our pack weren't right? Because I was revealing a vulnerability in caring?

Fuck that.

"A king shouldn't care about *all* his people?" I thundered, angry now.

"More like *why* do you care *now*?"

I stood, meaning to block her path. Her pacing was getting on my nerves. But instead, her body jolted in a new heat spasm. I felt the seductive waves of it even several feet away. And her scent flooded my senses again, making my cock stand to attention and my hips jut forward.

Mine. Mate. Breed.

"No, stay back!" Zelene held out a hand to ward me off. And I had half a mind to ignore it and pull her against me anyways. But then she added, "I need to figure this out. If you touch me, I'll lose all sense. My head will fill with hopes and fantasies of how things could be. Of a future I can't possibly have. So just... *stay back*. Because I need... I *need* to understand you."

I had the feeling it would take many, many years for us to understand each other. She'd lived a different life than me. But if it was clarity she wanted, I would fucking give it to her.

"My mother was an omega."

Zelene lifted her head to stare at me. "I know. Everyone knows the Queen was omega. But that was before The Division."

"Yes. But you don't know how she died."

"Sure, I do. She grew sick and couldn't be

healed. Even with new technology available."

I shook my head. Zelene knew what the pack had been told about the queen's death. But that story wasn't the truth.

I swallowed the ache in my throat.

"A lie. My father ordered that no one outside the two of us ever know the truth." And until now, I had kept this secret. "My mother was murdered during the Omega Wars."

"Just like mine," Zelene breathed.

"Her murderer, Garreth..." I spat his name like poison "... was an omega of power. My father's closest adviser and also my matron uncle."

"The queen was murdered by her own brother?" The horror in Zelene's voice echoed the feeling I'd kept in my heart all these years.

"I was only a youngling in my seventh year. Sometimes I try to remember what she looked like, but it was so long ago."

Zelene's hand fluttered to her throat while the other arm wrapped around her middle clenching in pain. Her heat was merciless, but she needed to hear this. Wanted to. And I wouldn't deny her.

"Garreth wanted unity with the humans. He thought diversity would make us a stronger people. And maybe he was right. But my father disagreed. He feared the humans only wanted us for our technology. They were desperate to survive after the Great Dust Storm. He thought when they discovered we were shifters, we'd be wiped out for being different." *The humans have a king of their own, his name is fear*, my father used to say. And he wasn't wrong. "Garreth was ordered to stand down. Instead, he betrayed our pack. He went to the humans and revealed what we are. The humans couldn't resist the allure of controlling beings who were part animal, and used Garreth to get close enough to launch a clandestine attack on the castle."

"The attack that started the Omega Wars. The very first."

I nodded. "They intended to take my father, knowing enough about our ways to understand the pack would scatter without their alpha. But instead, they found my mother alone in bed and took her hostage."

"Adalai..." The first time her lips uttered my name and it sounded like pure agony.

"They didn't make it past the castle guards. Garreth realized the mistake he'd made trusting the humans, but it was too late. My father's wolf tore the humans apart. All but one. The one who held a knife to my mother's throat."

I looked at Zelene, her eyes welling with tears for what she knew was coming. She was omega. And I'd spent a lot of my life calling her kind traitors. Betrayers. Spent a lifetime hating them. But in that moment, I couldn't hate her.

I couldn't hate any of them.

If Garreth had been a beta, it would be betas in the Badlands. If he'd been an Alpha, perhaps we'd have no king at all. Perhaps it would be me starving in the desert.

"My mother didn't make it. And neither did Garreth. The only survivor of that incident was my father. And you know what happened next."

"He declared war on the omegas."

I nodded. The first civil war of our kind. It had turned our best qualities into our worst. It separated us, made us enemies and lords. We called it a pack, but Zelene was right. We had become something else.

She shuddered out a breath. "Now, here you are, trapped with a woman you hate."

"Hate?" I drew her scent into my lungs feeling like it could make me invincible. "I don't hate you, Zelene." I took a step forward, backing her against the wall. *Touch, taste, prove.* My inner wolf pawed at my chest, bending me to its desires.

"You hate what I am."

My arm darted out, pulling her fast against my body as I pinned her to the wall with my hips, my hard cock sliding against her belly in warning.

"Maybe I did once upon a time."

She whimpered, fresh sweat coating her heat-riddled body, and writhed against me. *Yessss.*

"But now... now it's something else.

Something stronger than hate. Stronger than me or my will. My father created The Division out of hate. I am going to tear it down, *out of love.*"

I watched her expression crumple like a wall falling, brick by brick, to reveal a hidden garden, lush and vibrant with feeling. And it was there, that desire she talked about to have better, be better. Want better. There was so much love in her, hidden behind that wall. I wanted just a piece of it to be mine.

But she shook her head, an aching moan slipping from her lips as her nails dug into my shoulder.

"It's my heat."

I licked a path up her neck, stopping at her delicate ear to nip. "What about it?"

"It's causing you to say things you don't mean."

I had the inescapable need to prove myself to her. Shifting my hips, I aligned my cock with her entrance, relishing her helpless moan at the contact our bodies made.

"You'll learn quickly, my rose, I never say things I don't mean."

She shook her head, eyes landing everywhere except on me. "You won't feel this way when it's over."

"I will."

"You won't. I know you won't."

"How could you know?" I gripped her jaw to force her head against the wall and bring her gaze to mine. "How could you possibly know how I feel about you? How you've turned me inside out. How you've given me something to look forward to when things seemed bleak. You've given me *hope*. So, you go ahead, let your head fill with those fantasies of a better life. Because I'm going to give it to you. And you will give me the same." Tears breached the rims of her eyelids to streak down her cheek and land on my fingers. "You'll be fully mine before we leave this bunker, female. And nothing will change it. No law, no army. Nothing. You said it before... I am the fucking king. *And I will have my queen.*"

With a hard thrust, I slammed into her as I took her lips, kissing her scream of relief away.

And again, we were one.

***

The darkness surrounded me in the bunker as I lay sprawled across the nest of blankets and pillows we'd used to rut upon. Zelene snored softly against my chest, her heat pangs sated for now.

It had been a long, sweaty day of mating, of making sure her body took as much of my seed as possible, as much pleasure as possible. But if she woke now and needed me again, I'd fuck her like a fresh male just coming into his alpha year. She'd made me a slave to her, and I couldn't remember what life was like before. Before the ballroom and the heat and this fucking bunker.

I grinned at the invisible ceiling above, grateful she wasn't awake to see me. Every single one of her pleasured moans and squeals was like a new dawn. We might as well have known each other a lifetime after this.

142

My smile faded as my mind turned to what life would be like for us outside the bunker. When her heat was over. She thought I would change my mind about her, but reality was worse than that.

I had to figure out a way to bring down The Division without causing another civil war. For all my promises, I didn't have a clue how to make it happen. I only knew that I would, for her.

For *us*.

And for my baby that would be growing in her belly soon.

Yesss, my wolf rumbled.

While my mind grappled for a solution to our problems, the wind outside whipped at the hatch overhead and the whistle of air through a crack grabbed my attention. Tavia had brought food earlier, and I'd given the whole meager offering to Zelene. My animal would take care of me until her heat broke and I could get us proper food.

But... the wind. Perhaps Tavia hadn't shut the hatch properly. If wind was getting inside the bunker that meant my omega's scent could escape and draw other males.

As if on cue, the sound of a wolf howling sent a chill of warning down my spine. Carefully, I slid away from Zelene and she moaned at the movement, her legs twisting apart like she was ready for me again. "Shh, rose."

The howling drew closer and I tipped my head, listening to confirm what my wolf was trying to tell me. What the animal had been trying to tell me all along. They were shifted. Fully shifted werewolves. More than one.

Wolves when there should be no wolves. Wolves who didn't suffer the same handicap those of us from the city did.

And they were coming for my queen.

Wolves, when she so easily denied the ability to shift. I knew it was a lie the moment it left her lips, but her secrets had to be earned.

Protect mate. My animal bucked and clawed inside, tearing at my humanity until my vision turned hot white.

The door to the bunker rattled and I sprung

from the bed just in time to watch it fly open, the wind nearly ripping it from the hinges. Before I could find my weapons, the heavy form of a man dropped down from the entrance, landing with a grunt as his boots hit the floor before standing to his full height. Even in the darkness, something about the man was familiar, but I didn't have time to figure it out. Another male was too fucking close to my naked mate. One who would hurt her. Another male was smelling her heat and wanting her and it was all too much.

My turn, my wolf seethed inside. *My turn to defend, to protect. To keep.*

No one would have her except me. And I would die before I let anyone hurt her.

The roar that came from within me was like nothing I'd ever heard before. My body rattled and shook as my inner animal clawed free. Bones twisted and popped forming the beast I'd always known was part of me but had never experienced. Smooth skin became ruffled fur. Fingers became razor sharp claws as I fell to the floor on all fours, unleashing a snarl.

Power. So much power flowed through me as my beast finally aligned with the man I'd always been. Lifting my head, I howled at the moon outside even though I couldn't see it in the confines of the bunker.

"A-Adalai," Zelene whispered. And her voice was like an arrow to my heart. Mine. *Mine*.

The intruder backed away, but made no move for the ladder.

"What... what the *fuck* have you done?" the intruder growled.

And that was when I recognized the man's voice.

Dagger.

I snarled a warning in my mind, instinct telling me he would hear it. *"Leave. Now. Before I kill you."*

Before Dagger could backtrack out of the bunker, another form made its way down the ladder, jumping from the lower rungs to the floor. And then Tavia's voice pierced the darkness.

"You *idiot*," she seethed. Through the dimness, I could see her angry scowl, narrowed on Dagger. "I told you, you couldn't come here. You led the wolves right to them. What were you thinking? Stupid, stupid alphas. You never listen—"

My growl pulled her attention away from Dagger, and she stared at my wolf form, her eyes so big the whites gleamed even in the dark. Her mouth opened but no words came. And before I could warn them back out the hatch, Zelene sprung from the bed to crouch in front of me. She pressed her front to my fur, her arms coming around my neck as she stared over her shoulder at the other two. A snarl curled her lip, throwing out a warning similar to mine.

"Go!" she said. "*Now*."

"We can't," Tavia argued. "The girls are dealing with the wolves this alpha brought down on you. We have to keep the hatch sealed until they're gone."

"You have to *go*," Zelene insisted. "I'm still in

heat. And the king... the king..." Her words faded out on a whimper and I was aware that she was growing needy again.

"Listen," Tavia held her hands out as if that would placate Zelene. "Everyone just... calm down. We're stuck here for a while, but as soon as the wolves are led away, we'll go." She looked at Dagger and he shook his head, expression still creased with disgust and surprise.

"I must speak to the king. *Alone*," he said.

"Not now," I snarled to let him know I disagreed. I wasn't leaving the bunker until Zelene's heat broke. And when that time came, I intended to rake his ass over the coals for disobeying my orders. No one was to leave the city.

No one.

"A new threat has been leveled on Luxoria, Your Majesty. One you're going to want to hear about." The tone of his voice made my instincts flare. Dagger didn't rile easily. And he didn't disobey. If he left the city against my orders, it

148

meant something was wrong.

Very wrong.

It meant whatever the human armies had cooked up this time, was bigger than anything we'd fought back before. And if the city was in danger... the Badlands were too. The pack, all of us, were in trouble.

I pressed into Zelene's body as if that could keep her from whatever danger was coming our way.

The obstacles were piling up, but it didn't change the way I felt.

If it was the last thing I did, I would keep my promise to my rose.

TEN
ZELENE

There was only one more day of my heat, and it threatened to kill us all. Adalai rumbled in his wolf form. He wasn't supposed to know we could shift. I'd betrayed every omega in the Badlands. As much as I wanted to believe the King would be my defender, I couldn't imagine what that meant for my sister, my friends, or the rest of the omegas.

"You should go," I said to Tavia. "The girls need you."

We'd been caught outside the bunker before when the wolves sensed our heat. Sometimes they knew even before we did, before our bodies warmed and the urges started. It took all of us to fight them off. If it was just Charolet and Ashla out there, they were in trouble. Rielle could be trapped in the castle, and if the Alphas knew where their king was, she might be in a totally different kind of danger.

"No way." Tavia crossed her arms over chest and glared at Adalai. I held him tighter, feeling more protective of him than my own sister. What had he done to me? "I'm not leaving you down here with a wolf. And a man who can't take his eyes off you because you're still in heat."

Dagger didn't shift his gaze away from me to refute her claim, but his lip curled in a growl I recognized. I'd seen him many times, but never this close. The alpha lord of the Badlands was disgusted to find his king extinguishing the heat of an omega.

Adalai growled low. Would he choose me over another alpha? "The king won't hurt me." My declaration earned a groan from my sister and the alpha. I wouldn't betray Adalai's trust and tell them what he'd said, moments after spilling his seed inside me. Neither Tavia nor his friend would believe it until they heard it from his lips.

I hated that. I hated that after the three incredible days we'd spent together, as one, he was still an alpha and I was an omega. That those words were still opposites, opposing forces. I groaned against his fur, and this fury had nothing to do with my heat. The declaration wouldn't mean anything until we got out of this bunker. Only his actions would make it more than an empty promise.

"We can't stay here," the alpha said. "The wolves will keep fighting until they get inside. It's not safe for us here, and your friends are in danger too."

"Like you care," Tavia scoffed.

"Brave little omega, when you stand in this bunker that reeks of Alpha seed and your dream of liberation."

Tavia took a step toward the Alpha. I remembered what Adalai said about bravery and stupidity, and hoped his friend agreed.

"When was the last time you defended yourself against an actual wolf?" She stared down the man. "Or were you so wrapped up in your own problems that you didn't know they existed, leaving us to fight that battle for you."

I gasped. But I couldn't tell Tavia that I lied to Adalai about the wolves. I hoped now that he'd shifted, he wouldn't remember that our stories didn't match.

"You have no idea what we do to keep you safe," the alpha roared.

"Enough!" Adalai put a stop to the pissing contest, his voice ringing through our minds even in his wolf form. *"Dagger is right. We're not safe here. We need to get back to the castle."*

Never had Adalai been more Alpha than he was at that moment. I pulled away from him as Tavia gasped. Even Dagger stepped back, like the King's power had given him a shove.

"King," I said softly. He didn't want me to call him that anymore, but our guests were in enough of an uproar without me calling His Majesty by his first name. "How will we get there?"

"Dagger will bring my men. Your friends know how to defend themselves against these aggressions. Once inside the castle, you'll have every protection afforded an Alpha."

"Have you lost your mind?" Dagger asked.

"No." Adalai pawed at the mattress. *"We've been fighting the wrong war for too long. The omegas have suffered enough for the actions of one man. They'll fight with us, if we give them reason to. Reward."*

Dagger scoffed. "They'll take your crown. Declare you unfit to lead."

"Who will? You?"

"My King, I swore I'd do whatever it takes to defend you and our city. I'm not sure what that means right now."

"Have you forgotten what you are? You're a pack animal. Pay attention to these omegas. How

they come together and fight. How they protect their own without any regard for the consequences."

My heart pounded, and that ever present heat intensified once again. It made me doubt what I heard. Did the king actually intend to liberate the omegas? And if he did, why did it scare me so much?

No matter what happened, everything about my life as I'd known it had changed. There was no way I could go back to the way I was before, an anonymous omega who worked in the castle kitchen. My sister had challenged this man named Dagger—someone who cared enough to come for the king—and that wasn't without its own consequences. And howls of wolves still swirled above us.

"I brought my gun," Dagger said. "Fully loaded with silver bullets. It will buy us a little space while we collect the omega females and bring them to safety inside the walls of the city."

"What will happen to them once they get

there?" They weren't safe among Alphas. We needed a guarantee of protection, or there was no reason for any of us to follow the King and Dagger.

"They'll come to the castle," Adalai said. *"Until we make an official declaration, we'll make sure they're safe."*

Dagger raised an eyebrow. "An official declaration about what?"

"The Division is over."

Tavia gasped, her gaze fixed on me, waiting for confirmation that what she heard was true. I shrugged.

"King, you don't know what you're saying—"

"Don't tell me what I know and what I don't!" Adalai lunged at Dagger. *"Get these females out of here, and ensure the safety of the others. We're going to the castle. Now."*

"She... she can't go like that." Tavia's body shook as hard as her voice. Omega wolves were bloodthirsty and vicious, just like everything else in the Badlands. Even escorted by Adalai and Dagger, there was no guaranteeing a safe and easy trip. "She's naked, smells like his seed, and is about to go into another wave of heat."

"Where are her clothes?" Dagger asked.

"My dress is ruined." I pressed my lips together to stifle a whine. The situation was dangerous enough already without me losing control of my senses and becoming more of a magnet for the wolves.

Dagger and Tavia groaned in unison. I didn't have to elaborate how the dress met its demise.

"My jacket." Adalai broke away from me and nudged the rich leather with his snout. *"She can wear that until we can have some proper clothes made for her."*

Tavia's mouth dropped at the implication.

"King, you're making a bold statement." Dagger scooped the jacket Adalai had worn to the celebration party off the filthy mattress. It was the only thing that would leave this bunker the same as it entered. "I'm begging you to think about this before we do something we can't change."

"I've been thinking about it ever since I laid

eyes on the female. Cover her with the jacket and bring us to the castle."

Dagger held the jacket out to me. My arms were wrapped tightly around my naked body. I wasn't so much ashamed to have him see me, but I was under the foolish assumption that I belonged to Adalai. He'd claimed my body every way possible, and made some strong declarations to me and to this alpha, but I knew as much as everyone else in this bunker that everything would change the moment we left this safe space.

Tavia took the jacket from him and draped it over my shoulders. It was lined with silk, and nothing so fine had ever touched my skin. Nothing but Adalai. She murmured for me to put my arms in the too long sleeves and encouraged me to stand. The jacket hit me at the knees. Tavia fastened the remaining buttons and smoothed her rough hands over the leather. There was no missing the tears in her eyes, but in the dark, I couldn't read her emotion.

"I...I don't know if I can do this." Another wave

of heat racked my body.

"You can. You have to." She'd uttered those words to me so many times, just like I'd done for her. It was the Badlands creed, especially as an omega female. "I'll carry you."

"*No,*" Adalai interrupted. *"She can ride on my back."*

"What if you have to fight, Your Majesty?" Tavia was so brave, questioning the king. "The wolves up there will stop at nothing to take a female in heat. They won't care that the king has claimed her as his."

Dagger sighed. "The omega is right. We need every advantage to ensure our safe passage. All we have is my gun. I can summon the guards, but I couldn't bring them with me because I wasn't sure how to explain that their leader was in the Badlands, rutting with an omega."

"You forget who you are," Adalai said. *"You don't have to explain anything to anyone. We make the rules, we can change them."*

My heart fluttered, hearing my words roll off

his lips in such an official capacity. For the first time, I believed that I could actually be his queen.

ELEVEN
ADALAI

I raced across the desert with Zelene on my back and Dagger at my side. The crazed howling of male wolves followed, gaining on us. Tavia had shifted and was nearby, in her wolf form. I could sense her trying to find the other two female omegas. Instinct told me that if we could get close enough to them, they would know to follow us to the city. Dagger had already alerted the border guards that we were coming, but they wouldn't be expecting me in my wolf form.

Would it change things?

No. I was king, and it was even more

important that I hold that position now, with so much at stake. A broken pack to put back together. A mate to treasure and care for. My prince in her belly. If he wasn't there yet, he would be soon. I'd see to it. And they would be fucking safe, if it was the last thing I did in this world. Her and her family and every other omega who wanted the pack to be one again.

Dagger knew the truth now. It was easier than I'd thought to declare my intentions to one of my most trusted men. But how would it be to declare it to the entire pack. And what kind of threat would the omega males be to the city now? I had no idea if they would happily come back under the protection of their King Alpha, or if they'd rebel even more. I didn't know if they could be trusted or if I'd have to wield my authority like a weapon.

But none of that mattered now. First, I needed to see that the females were safe. Then I would handle my people and the laws.

Zelene's arms tightened around my neck as I

powered across the dry sand, kicking up a cloud of dust. The heat from her pussy scalded my back where she tried not to writhe. I could tell she ached and my wolf wanted to halt everything and tend to her, but it was too dangerous.

Soon. Soon we would be back to the castle and I'd soothe her. And she would soothe me.

That was it, wasn't it? That was exactly what my omega did for me. My entire life, I'd felt the jagged edges that made up my soul, my being. I'd known they were there, and accepted them. Accepted the feeling of incompleteness that plagued us all, and blamed it on not being able to shift.

But it wasn't *just* my animal that I'd needed. I had been missing the other half of me, my mate. And now I'd found her. She filled in the rough spots so that I could be whole.

I thought of my father and mother as I ran across the dry land. It made sense that my father had turned so cold after losing her. Without her, he was something else entirely. It made sense why he'd demanded a separation, even if it was the wrong thing to do.

And it made sense that I be the one to bring us all back together.

The king I was before Zelene, couldn't have done that. But who I was *now*... that was who I was meant to be.

A vicious roar hit my ears—close enough that the sound wasn't only in my mind—and I knew we weren't going to make it across the Badlands without a fight. Pulling to a stop, I slid Zelene off my back, while Dagger and Tavia surrounded her. Together we formed a shield, and just in time as one by one, snarling omega wolves prowled over the sand toward us.

Zelene let off a pained whimper and I felt her heat pulse in the air. "Adalai..." Her voice was thin with warning. The close proximity of the other males was making her worse.

"Don't shift," Tavia's voice ricocheted through our minds. *"Whatever you do, Zee, you cannot shift."*

"Why?" Dagger asked.

"If she shifts, her wolf will be in charge," she answered. *"And with the heat, she will likely fight us to get to a male."*

I let off a thunderous growl. *"Over my dead fucking body."*

"No," Zelene panted. "No, I won't. I want... *Adalai.* Adalai is mine."

Her declaration appeased me, but only a little.

"Don't shift," Tavia repeated, her tone firm in my head.

The omega wolves moved closer as my mind worked to come up with a solution for fighting them off. But there were so many of them. Twenty. Maybe thirty. They were their own pack of snarling rabid beasts, and they wanted only one thing.

They wanted what was *mine.*

Unacceptable.

There was only one thing to do. One course to take.

My wolf pawed the sand as a threatening

snarl rolled up my chest and through my fangs.

Kill them all.

I lunged at the closest wolf, going for his neck, while Dagger used his gun to battle back others who were too brave for their own good. Behind me, I could hear Tavia's wolf barking her warnings to the males who got too close to Zelene. But the omegas didn't stop progressing. Soon, she would have to fight too, and my rose would be on her own.

One by one, I battled the approaching wolves. With Dagger by my side, we pushed them back. And each yelp as my fangs pierced fur and skin was an indescribable satisfaction. *The blood of my enemies…*

"No." The voice was faint, but I would hear her over the roar of a crowd any day. "*No*," Zelene cried, "don't kill them."

Don't kill them? They wanted to take her from me, and she begged for mercy?

"*Don't listen to her,*" Tavia said. "*Kill them, or they will kill you.*"

168

"They aren't your enemies," Zelene argued. "How... how will you bring us together... if... *mmm*... if we keep fighting?"

"Rose, they want to hurt you," I thundered, growling around the throat of the male I'd pinned.

A wolf lunged from the side, and the only warning I had before his fangs ripped into my flank was Zelene's horrified gasp. I roared, releasing the other wolf, and turned to the one who attacked me. Dagger was there, to fight back the others and Tavia dove for one sneaking in from the side.

But it was futile.

There were too many.

Too many heat crazed males. Too many angry over who I was. Too many, and too powerful.

Zelene's scream ripped through the air, thick with pheromones, but the fighting continued. Blood soaked my fur, and I didn't know if it was mine or not. Only that I wanted to spill as much of it as possible before I fell.

In my head, I heard new voices...

"The males are out of control. Protect the king and his mate."

"Fight our own? We can't do that."

"Do you want peace? If you do, protect the king. Protect his mate. It's the only way."

I didn't recognize the voices but they didn't mean to harm Zelene and that was all that mattered.

Little by little the omega wolves began to still, even if their growls didn't settle. Some of them even backed away. Tavia went quiet, and Dagger straightened to look around, his eyes going wide at what he saw.

Pulling myself away from the male wolf I'd been about to kill, I took in the scene. Wolves had surrounded Zelene, but not the males we'd been fighting back. These were female omegas. So many of them, I couldn't see where they ended. They stood tall and proud and vicious, reminding me of what Zelene said about the way they watched out for each other in the Badlands. I knew my rose was just like these females. If she wasn't crippled by her heat, she'd be standing fierce beside me to protect what needed protecting.

A true queen.

And the way her pack of females came together for her now... this was the key to protecting our people. Together, as one. Not divided as we had been for so long.

I stood on my injured leg, putting less weight on that paw, and stared down the remaining males who eyed my mate. They wouldn't dare make a move for her now, but I knew what had to be done, and none of them—male or female— were going to like it.

The alpha must demand submission.

Lifting my face to the sky, I let my instincts guide me. From deep in my gut, the sound rose, rumbling forth in a commanding howl to the moon. The cry was loud in my ears, reminding me of my father's alpha call. It had been so long since I'd heard it, that I almost forgot what it sounded like. But I could never forget the way it rolled down my spine, a heavy weight, even as a child in my human form. The way it urged me down, to the floor before his feet. The way it demanded my supplication and reminded me I wasn't in charge.

Bow. "*Bow to your king*," I resonated in their minds.

I let off another bellow, not waiting to see if the first one brought them all down. No matter what my omega mate said, if they couldn't bow to the alpha, they wouldn't be part of the pack. One straggler had caused my mother's demise. I wouldn't let the same thing happen to Zelene.

Bow to your alpha king.

When the moon had thoroughly heard my call, I looked to my people. Many cowered, the alpha call affecting them in a similar way Zelene's heat affected me. Whimpers of defeat rolled through my mind, but still some didn't lower themselves.

I turned to eye the omega females, including my own who was already on her knees. "*Bow*," I demanded. And one by one they bent to the ground, uttering their allegiance. Then I faced the males. *"Bow, and you will live."*

Dagger lowered his knee first, but not for the first time. The omega males followed his lead. Some of the pledges I heard in my head were even grateful. How long had they fought amongst themselves with no one but Dagger to direct them? I would be a good king to them, I vowed to myself. Not just for Zelene or the pack, but for who my father could have been had he not been so lost.

I went to my mate, careful not to show my limp. No weakness would be tolerated while the omegas were learning their place. Nudging her with my nose, I pushed her up. She wouldn't bow to me anymore. Not unless it was in our bed.

"This is your queen," I thundered, emphasizing the declaration with another alpha call. *"You will not harm her. Any who move upon her will suffer death at my hands."*

Tears streamed down Zelene's face but I couldn't tell if it was because of my words or because she was in pain.

It was time to go.

"Climb on, my rose."

"You're hurt," she whispered, but I growled her concern away and bumped her knees with my body so that she fell onto my back.

The battle was only halfway won. There was still work to do. But for now, the omegas understood that change was coming.

With a final nod to the wolves, I headed for the city gates with Dagger and my mate's family in tow.

TWELVE
ZELENE

This time, I paid her in gold. As queen, I didn't have to buy my own fabric. I should've had an omega do that for me. But everything was different now, and I intended to show my people that not only through my words but also by my actions. Words didn't matter, they could be bent, twisted, and broken. I would let what I did speak for me.

My intention was to lift everyone in this city off their knees so we could stop fighting each other and focus on the real enemies. The humans. And I'd start with the woman who set everything into motion, the one who'd sold me that beautiful pink and gold fabric even though she knew I'd lied to her.

Did I, though? Because now the castle was my home.

I'd never give her another reason to doubt me again.

"I knew you were capable of great things," she said as she snipped the last thread and stepped back to admire her handiwork. She had made me another pink dress. This one, the color of rose petals. She met my gaze. "That was why I sold you the fabric. And instead of getting yourself killed for having something that shouldn't have belonged to you, you did something beautiful with it."

Looking a queen directly in the eye and speaking her mind like that would've had serious consequences for an omega just weeks ago. But once Adalai and I returned to the castle, we had a serious talk. He'd been a wolf, in the heat of the moment, when he said The Division was over. At

JAMESON | STRASSEL

the time, I'd been consumed by instinct and need, and it was imperative that we be on the same page. The lives of my fellow omegas depended on it, and I refused to turn my back on them because I had a chance to better myself. No. It might have been every wolf for themselves in the Badlands during The Division, but that wasn't what any of us wanted. I couldn't forget the way the mass of omega females came together to help me in the desert. From here out, I would treat every omega the way I treated Tavia, Charolet, Rielle, and Ashla. Our elders told stories of how we had all worked together to fight for what was ours. My mother died fighting for that very principle.

I wouldn't let any of it be in vain.

"You look gorgeous, Zelene." Tavia was breathtaking herself. Her dark hair had been swept up on her head and she wore a robin's egg blue gown.

"So do you. You all do," I said, finding the others. "It's like you stepped out of my dream."

Charolet stood behind Tavia, wearing green

chiffon, and wiggling her freshly manicured fingers in front of her face. "Never thought I'd have these." The manicurist had glued little jewels to their fingernails and mine were painted the deep pink of my original dress. Our hair was done too, twisted into decorative curls and bejeweled with crystals. Later I would wear a crown.

A crown. Me. Zelene from the Badlands. Holy crap.

Rielle was decked out in purple, and Ashla's dress was gold. No bland and rough sugar sack cotton for these ladies ever again.

"Are you nervous, Zee? Going in front of all the people of the city and the Badlands for the first time?" Ashla asked. She hadn't stopped fluttering her eyelashes since the makeup artist left. My friends, now my court, had always been beautiful. It took my breath away to see them get the respect they deserved.

"I'm absolutely terrified." The butterflies rose in my belly, but they were different than the night I crashed the party at this castle. For the first time since The Division, omegas, betas, and alphas would be standing together, equal, watching Adalai promise himself to me forever.

There had been rumblings loud enough to penetrate the thick stone walls of the castle that some people in the city, and some in the Badlands too, thought he'd made a mistake. As the story spread, they decided I was too reckless and too inexperienced to lead. Even other omegas worried that the betas and alphas wouldn't respect me.

"It doesn't matter what I say when we go out on the balcony. I'll show them Adalai made the right choice by being true to my heart, day after day."

"It still freaks me out that you call him Adalai. I keep expecting to get chased out of here," Rielle said with a chuckle. "Like I'm going to wake up from this dream, back in the Badlands, dirty, hungry, and late for work in the downstairs kitchen."

"Never again." Tonight, they'd sit at the head

table with the king and all his most trusted alphas. Alphas that were hungry for mates of their very own. I hoped like Adalai, they wanted to do the right thing. Because I would never stop being fiercely protective of my girls. "You're part of my court now. Everything is different."

"That's what scares me," Charolet said under her breath. She didn't mean for me to hear it, but she didn't shy away from my gaze when I did. "I'm afraid they'll try to divide us, and make the castle crumble from inside the walls. I don't know what it takes to be in the Queen's Court."

"I don't know what it means to be queen." The door opened, and one of Adalai's castle staff motioned to us that it was time to go. "But we're about to find out."

"Zelene," Tavia called to me before I left the room. Her eyes shone with unshed tears. "I know Mom's looking down on you from heaven and smiling, getting all the other omegas up there together and pointing at you saying, that's *my* girl."

I'd done what Mom couldn't. I'd convinced the King Alpha to end The Division. But I couldn't think about how much we'd had to sacrifice to get to this very place right now or I'd lose it.

"But are you sure about this?" Tavia added. "That you want to marry Adalai?"

"Of course I am. I love him." New butterflies fluttered in my belly. It was the first time I'd said those words out loud. "It changes everything for all of us." My sister swallowed hard, but her gaze didn't waver from mine. "Things can never go back to the way they were."

"That's a good thing." I understood what she meant. We may have been filthy and starving, but we weren't broken. We didn't know what changes my marriage would bring to the lives of the people we cared about. The fight didn't end when the crown rested on my head. No. It had just begun.

My legs were jelly and my head swam as I followed the women through the winding hallways of the castle. I was more nervous tonight than I had been the night of the party. As an unruly omega, I had nothing to lose. Now all the people of our pack, our divided city, depended on me. I gave them hope that things could finally turn around. That the wars could end and we could work together again in peace.

I arrived in the grand court, the same room that had hosted the military party. Adalai looked absolutely gorgeous, framed by the lamps that illuminated the balcony. He wore a rich silk jacket of navy blue. The sleeves had been embroidered with gold and his chest was decorated with too many war medals to count. His onyx eyes sparkled when he saw me, and he held out his hand.

"Her Majesty." The words were little more than a hot breath against my ear, but they sent a shiver down my spine. He pressed his lips against my cheek, steadying me. "I've dreamed of this moment, when I would present my queen to a united city. But never did I imagine a beauty as splendid as you."

His words made my chest warm with emotion.

"I hope to do you proud, my King." I curtsied. Not in a submissive move, it was pure respect. I'd worried that once my heat passed and Adalai was no longer ruled by his long-dormant animal, he would realize what he'd done. Ended The Division and taken an omega as his bride. But he had absolutely no regrets about his decision. He immediately set this celebration into motion, because he couldn't wait to present me to the city.

Except I feared we weren't prepared. There was still so much I had yet to share with the king about the Badlands. His mother's murder had triggered The Division, and he had lost all touch with that side of him. It was up to me to educate him, and keep both the alphas and omegas safe. Not to mention, the random missing omegas nobody could account for. Their families would want the king to care, to take action to find them.

Like everything else in my life, I didn't know

how I'd do it yet, but I knew I could pull it off. "They can't wait to meet you," Adalai said. "They've been calling your name. Wait until they see you. You look absolutely stunning. You've made me proud to call you my Queen."

"I'm still an omega," I reminded. "I always have been, and I always will be. That's how I plan to   rule." "You'll bring justice to people who are starving for it. You'll be the reason we win the war against the humans and get our Luxoria back." He put his hand on the small of my back. The heat from his body seeped through the thick velvet. "Come with me."

A cheer rose from the crowd when the king and I stepped out onto the balcony. He squeezed my hand in his and then raised them high between us. Unity. Pride. Strength.

Dagger stepped onto the balcony behind us. He put his hand on Adalai's shoulder. "It's time for the ceremony, Your Majesty."

Adalai turned toward me, kissing me to the

approval of the crowd...well, most of them anyway. I could've sworn I heard a few boos. But I didn't let it bother me. I wouldn't be the most popular queen, not yet. I had a lot to prove. Every day of my life had been a battle, and I'd survived so far. I'd been preparing for this uphill crawl my entire life.

Standing between us in his military dress leather, Dagger crossed his hands low on his belly. He nodded to me. "Your Majesty." No hiding the words still tasted bitter on his tongue. He'd lost all control of the Badlands at the hands of a renegade queen. "It's my honor to welcome you to the court."

"I look forward to serving you."

Dagger stepped up to the microphone. "Today is a day that some among us have dreamed of, and yet... others have feared with all their hearts—"

"What the fuck?" Adalai muttered under his breath. "I gave him the vows. How dare he go off script."

I leaned close, because I was shaking and I wasn't sure I was able to whisper. "If he means to cause a riot, let him. He can get it all out of his system, but we *will* bring the people of the Luxoria together once and for all."

"—The end of The Division. We have fought long and hard. Some have given their lives, and lost loved ones. But perhaps we all wanted the same thing." Dagger looked down at a slip of paper. The vows? His lip turned up at the corner as he continued. "Peace. Today is the ultimate symbol of that transition. The union between King Adalai of Luxoria, and omega Zelene. This is a day that our descendants will read about in history books, as life as we know it will never be the same."

Dagger shot a hard gaze my direction. His words were the same as Tavia's, but they held a vastly different meaning.

Adalai growled and a gasp rolled over the crowd. "Are these wedding vows or a statement of mutiny?"

Dagger blinked before meeting Adalai's glare. "Just stating facts, Your Majesty."

"State them elsewhere, if you must. This is my fucking mating ceremony," the king hissed low.

Dagger clenched his jaw, clearly considering his next move. Zelene let out a breath when he leaned forward to the microphone. "Do you have anything you'd like to say to your bride before promising yourself to her forever?"

"Yes." Adalai sighed deeply, trying to shake off the exchange, as he turned to me. "My beautiful Zelene, my rose. I knew the moment I laid eyes on you that I was meant to be yours forever... even if all I wanted to do was make you mine. I didn't know who you were, or what you risked to come to me. Only that you were the answer to a question I never knew I had, and I'd go to any lengths to have you. I couldn't have guessed how you would change the lives of everyone in the city. I'm excited for our pack—alpha, beta, *and* omega—to get to know you, and for you to have a chance to make their lives better. I can't wait for them to see you like I have. Smart. Brave. Caring. And just."

His loving words stole my breath as he placed the crown on my head. Solid gold and bejeweled, it surprised me with its weight. Then he leaned in and kissed my forehead. A chaste move meant to win over the crowd in my favor. He'd save the fire for when we were alone.

It was my turn to speak to the crowd for the first time. "Your Majesty. You told me not to call you that anymore, but you truly are magic. There was no way you didn't know what I was when you met me, with my bare feet and dirty skin. But still, you were willing to give me a chance. You listened to me like I was your equal. That's the sign of a great leader. I can't wait to spend the rest of my life with you, and help you serve all the people of this great city."

Another cheer rose from the crowd as I took Adalai's face in my hands and kissed him. Even in heels, I had to go up on my tiptoes to meet his lips. It was so easy to forget anyone else was there, until Dagger cleared his throat.

"Would you like to say anything to the people of the city, Queen Zelene?"

That title would take some getting used to.

"I would." I stepped up to the microphone, overwhelmed by the response of the crowd. Even from this vantage point, I saw so many familiar faces. They were still dressed in the plain wardrobe of the Badlands residents, but the hopeful expression they held was a shocking change to their appearance. They saw themselves in me, standing on that balcony in the gorgeous velvet gown.

"Hi." My message was mostly for the omegas, and I wanted to make sure they knew that. No fancy language was necessary. "Never in my wildest dreams did I think I'd be standing here, addressing you from the castle as your queen. And believe me, I've had some wild dreams. When you look at me, with my pretty dress, crown, and fancy title, I don't want you to see any of that. I want you to see yourself. I want you to see Zelene who worked in the kitchen of this very castle ever since she was old enough to see over the counter. Zelene who fought to keep her friends safe in the Badlands. Because I want you to know I'll fight just as hard for you. Whatever lies ahead, Luxoria and the Badlands fighting together will be unbeatable, and I am humbled for the opportunity to serve as your queen."

Adalai's hand was at the small of my back again, his lips against my ear. "You're a natural leader."

I turned away from the crowd. The celebration had already started in the city streets. A band played as fireworks exploded in my honor. It was completely overwhelming.

"I'm used to doing things scared," I said.

"You don't need to worry about that anymore. You're mine now. To protect and keep, and I plan on taking my vows seriously." Adalai led me away from the balcony. His men waited for him, as well as my ladies.

My court.

Without these ladies, I'd never be here. I stopped and hugged all of them, and wiped away their tears, even if I was pretty sure they were happy ones.

I wanted to be alone with my king. It was harder than ever now, with courtesans and support staff—they were no longer referred to as servants—everywhere we turned. But tonight, they wanted to celebrate too.

Past the winding staircase, the upper floor was quiet, insulated from the celebration below. The castle had stood for centuries, a testament to shifter power, even if the occupants of the city hadn't been able to shift for too long.

Our bedroom was at the end of the hall. It was the first night we'd spend together in it. My sister was the one who insisted we stay apart until we were officially King and Queen. At the time, I hated it but I'd thank her later. Anticipation had been building inside me, much like my heat, but this time it was something I could totally control.

Adalai shut the door behind us. "You were

amazing out there."

"Thank you." I closed my eyes for a long blink. My knees were doing that knocking thing again. "And I know you'll be amazing in here."

"Come here, Your Majesty," he growled, and I did as my king told me. "Turn around and let me help you out of your pretty dress."

"Careful," I warned. "Edythe, my seamstress, gave this thing a hundred little buttons."

Adalai snickered. "She's probably getting me back for her experience so far in the Badlands."

"She's on payroll now, because I want her to make all the dresses for me and the girls." I couldn't wait until my sister and all my friends had a chance to feel like I did today. They might not get an official title like I did, but I could make sure the sun, moon, and stars revolved around them for at least one day.

Cool air hit my back as he worked slowly, methodically not to ruin Edythe's handiwork. "You can have everything you want."

It was a heady feeling, to know I would never

suffer, never want for anything again. But so many omegas in the Badlands would go to bed tonight without that guarantee. "I want the omegas to be safe."

"They will be." His lips were on my shoulder, kissing me as he pushed the dress down my body. I carefully stepped out of it, picked it up, and placed it on a chaise. It was the nicest thing I'd ever worn, besides the crown, and I wouldn't leave it on the floor.

Adalai grinned at me. "Leave the crown on, Your Majesty."

I nodded, walking over to him in nothing but my lacy corset, panties, and impossibly high heels. I'd spent the night before my mating ceremony with my girls trying to learn how to walk in them. They might be the next thing I made a rule about—that no woman had to wear heels ever again.

My king spun me around to the bed. I sank into it as he lay me down. So much softer than the ratty old mattress in the bunker that he'd taken me against during my heat. Snapping the corset open with as much care as he had done with my dress, I was almost bare before him. And he was wearing way too many clothes.

I wasn't in heat anymore, but I was hot and hungry for this man. The man I loved.

My hands trembled as I reached for him, but Adalai shook his head. I may be queen now, but he would always be my alpha. He unbuttoned his jacket, and lay it beside my dress. Those medals were just as important to him as the gown was to me. They both symbolized sacrifice and victory. He stepped out of his pants, his cock hard and ready for me. My inner muscles pulsed as I craved having it inside.

Adalai's gaze raked over my body, and settled on my stomach with a furrowed brow. The mattress shifted under the weight of his knee when he joined me on the bed. Pushing a few stray hairs away from my face, his fingers settled on my lips. I was hungry for him, and I coaxed him inside. He thrust inside my mouth, fucking it with his fingers. I took him deep as I could, a prelude of what was to come.

He ran his other hand over my breasts, and I bowed off the bed, almost biting his fingers when he pinched my nipple.

Our lips met in a kiss that wasn't like any of the others. This one was pure magic, there was no king, no queen, no alpha, no omega. We'd come together as one.

We separated with a gasp, and Adalai pushed my legs apart. I was so ready for him, and his fingers glided over my slick, swollen folds. He plunged inside me, making my hips rise off the bed.

"I didn't think it was possible for you to be more beautiful—" He startled at the banging on the door. "Fuck," he said under his breath.

"You don't have to answer it," I called after him as he hopped into his pants. I pulled the satin comforter over my body, since he actually planned to open the door. "You're the king."

"That's exactly why I have to answer it." The

words were tipped with a growl.

For the first time since we left the bunker, I felt like an omega. Like whatever business waited on the other side of that door was more important than me. Before the interruption, I'd truly felt like a queen and it humbled me to realize how far I had to fall.

"Your Majesty." Dagger was breathless in the doorway, his brow furrowed in anger. "I apologize for the interruption." His cheeks pinked when he caught sight of me on the bed.

"This better be fucking good," Adalai snarled.

"The human army has infiltrated the city."

My stomach took a dive at the news, and I sat forward.

"How?" Adalai roared. He stormed away from the door, grabbing his jacket but slamming it down on the chaise again.

"We don't have intelligence on that yet, sir. We think the guards got too caught up in the wedding celebration—"

"I'm the only one who needs to be celebrating.

The goddamned betas can wait one fucking night so I can be with my mate." Adalai's voice reverberated on the stone walls. It was a miracle fur hadn't broken through his skin. His animal was close to the surface. I could sense it like it was my own.

"You're still in charge of the Badlands, Dagger." Adalai added, sounding a little calmer. "It's the first line of protection for the city. Your omegas should have stopped the army."

"Maybe they're not ready to fight for you after all," Dagger said softly, his gaze falling to me, but the blush was replaced by a condescending smirk. Like it was him and not me who wore a crown on their head. "Maybe your queen was sent to you as a distraction, a gateway to anarchy—"

"No!" It was my turn to roar. "I want nothing more than to bring this city together, and to end the suffering of my people."

"Your people," Dagger mocked. "You're awfully selfless as you lay naked on the king's bed, the room smelling of sex—"

"Enough!" Adalai slammed his fist against the wall. His eyes were on fire as he looked between me and Dagger. Like he was trying to decide which one of us to believe.

My breath caught in my throat. My days of feeling like I was less than anyone else were supposed to be over. I lifted my chin in challenge. If Adalai took Dagger's theory over everything we had together, and tossed me back into the Badlands like omega garbage, he'd experience what it was truly like to have a mutiny on his hands. Because I'd be the one leading it. High heels, disgraced crown, and all.

Adalai knelt on the bed beside me, his voice quiet and harsh. "My rose, did someone send you to me? Did someone buy you that dress and help you gain access to the victory celebration?"

Dagger scoffed. "You probably should've asked her this before you gave her the crown."

My animal was going crazy inside me. "Tell him to stop. This is absurd. I don't deserve this." It was possible my moments as queen were numbered, and I planned to take advantage of every single one of them.

Adalai gnashed his teeth, but finally stood tall, turning to Dagger. "Zelene is your queen and you'll treat her as such." He pointed at the floor. "On your knees with your apology."

Dagger hesitated, like he expected the king to take it back.

"Now, or I'll give you to the humans as a peace offering."

He got down on his knees, bowing deeply. "Your majesty, I misspoke. Please forgive the indiscretion."

"You'll be forgiven when you show me that you view the omegas as equals, not as a threat." I turned to Adalai. "To answer your question, no one sent me to you. I kept my plan a secret until the last minute. I never meant to find you. I only hoped to find a beta who could overlook who I really was. I starved myself to save for the dress, and Tavia begged me not to come to the party, because she knew it would bring us nothing but trouble." I went to my knees on the mattress, trying to meet him eye to eye so he could read the truth in me. "Was she right? Was this a mistake?" He didn't answer. "There's no mutiny. She was my reason. I did it for her. Because she'd been fired from her job at the castle. Disgraced. Without her income, as meager as it was, we wouldn't have survived. I couldn't risk her working further south. What if she was kidnapped like the others? I'd never forgive myself."

I rose from the bed. My new wardrobe had been brought here, but I had no idea where it was. And something told me it wasn't exactly appropriate for battle.

"You need to leave, Dagger. Now. Ready your men—all your men—for battle. Ladies too if they care to join." My voice shook as I gave the powerful alpha orders. "But make no mistake, everyone has a role in keeping every inch of this city safe. That includes the Badlands."

"You're going to let her give orders?" Dagger eyed Adalai, like I wasn't even in the room.

"She's the queen, and this city is under attack. For you to question her orders is to undermine me," Adalai said, but his voice was uncertain. If I could hear it, so could his captain. "You heard your queen. Go."

With a sigh, Dagger stormed toward the door, slamming it shut behind him.

"Why would you question me? Especially in front of Dagger, who already thinks I'm a traitor."

"The attack caught us all by surprise. He's a good man—"

"You're avoiding my question. And taking Dagger's word over mine. He was the one hinting at mutiny as he read our wedding vows." I doubted everything, and Tavia's words rang clear in my head. *It changes everything for all of us.* The omegas would be forced into battle tonight to defend a city that had brought them nothing but pain before we had a chance to prove things would be different for them. Better. I had to lead them. But more than that, I had to make sure Adalai still believed in me.

How could we be shaken this easily, when we'd just vowed to respect each other for eternity?

Adalai steeled himself, all business. All royalty. "It's the timing, to be honest, Zelene. Ending the Division should've made Luxoria stronger, not more susceptible to attack. Yet, instead of spending the night making love to you, I'm forced to lead a battle."

"Yes, the timing is suspect." For Dagger, not the omegas. He'd been in charge of the Badlands and had been content to let us suffer. I did worry the omegas would hesitate to take his command out of sheer pride, knowing nothing of the suspicions that had arose from this conversation. Not having any idea they could be sacrificing their omega queen. I had to speak for them. It was my time to lead. "The last thing omegas want is more fighting. More war."

I took a couple cautious steps toward Adalai. I'd do anything to get that feeling back, just before Dagger sent my building orgasm spiraling into a deep, dark abyss. "We want peace. Everything I told you before is true."

"In the bunker, you lied to me about shifting."

"I was scared. I didn't know you yet. If it were only me, I would have spoken the truth. But telling you then could have ruined the people I love."

"And now? Would you speak the truth now, to the one you *claim* to love?"

Claim. Was he really saying what I thought he was saying?

I swallowed down the sick ache in my middle. My heart was breaking and I didn't have time to let it. There was a battle to fight. A city to protect. A people to unite. Maybe I would always have to prove myself. Even to him. The king. The one who knew me on a deeper level than anyone else ever could.

I lifted my chin, blinking back the tears that threatened to fall. "We want to see Luxoria back to its glory days. Back to when our mothers were both alive. The omegas will fight for you, Adalai, and this city. All they want is a chance. Will you give them that chance?"

He eyed me, his expression stony for too long before he let off a hard sigh.

"Come, rose. We have work to do."

It wasn't exactly an answer. But it was all I would get for now. I just hoped the omegas trusted me more than Adalai did.

THIRTEEN
ADALAI

Perched atop the city walls to gauge the melee below, my emotions were at war. Dagger was right to doubt Zelene. After all, hadn't my father been betrayed by one of his most trusted? It was Dagger's responsibility to question things. But his suggestion that my mate could be a traitor made me want to rip his fucking throat out.

My heart screamed that she would never do this, put the city in danger to bring the omegas up. But my training, the years of my father's soured words, planted doubt in my mind.

Shit.

I glanced away from the battle below to stare at her. *Mine*. My rose. Would she do this?

No, my wolf howled inside.

I watched Zelene pace the small walkway above the city. She chewed nervously at her thumbnail. "How did they get past the omegas?" she muttered low. As if to answer her question, vicious twin roars split the air, drawing our gazes out to the desert.

What I saw there froze my feet to the stone. "What the *fuck*..."

Just past the city gates, I could see so many of our omegas in their wolf form, all of them focused on two monstrosities that couldn't be named, the army humans forgotten. The beasts stood at least eight feet tall, on muscular hind legs that resembled those of a wolf, but their bodies, their thick chests and arms, took on a human form. Most alarming were their faces. Covered in fur with glowing eyes, snarling so I could see their fangs even from far away. When they howled at the moon, I felt it in my bones, vibrating with the same demand my father's roar used to have.

And that meant every other shifter felt it too. Every alpha, beta, and omega.

The alpha inside me growled low. *I should be down there, challenging them.*

My omega wolves charged the beasts, attacking to defend the Badlands, and it wasn't lost on me that none of my alpha commanders were down there. No one was helping the omegas. As if nothing had changed at all. As if me taking one as my beloved made no difference.

Anger flared in my chest, hot and furious.

Zelene muttered something under her breath but I didn't hear it through the roar of my animal wanting out. I stared at her. The look of worry in her eyes screamed at me to do something. "... missing omegas," she said, "half shifted... the humans have done something to them..."

Missing omegas.

Were those monsters the ones Zelene told me about in the bunker? The ones who disappeared under my watch. If it was true... the humans had turned them into weapons. Because as I listened to my mate piece things together beside me, I watched my omegas fall, one by one, at the hands of two hulking beasts that seemed to have no weaknesses. Blood sprayed as they slashed at wolves with their clawed human hands, kicking their way through the pack of omegas.

One omega turned his attention away from the beasts. He looked toward the castle, his eyes finding me at the top of the wall. I was frozen in his stare for several breaths until he sent up a wailing cry to the moon above. The howl caused other omegas to stop their fight and look to the castle.

I knew what this was. They were asking their king for help. And maybe they didn't think it would matter. Maybe they thought they were still on their own. But hadn't I made them promises in the desert when Zelene was aching from her heat. Hadn't I promised to do better?

It could be a trap.

Before my eyes, I watched one beast sink his

claws into the howling omega. Blood soaked the sand, glistening under the moonlight.

"Adalai!" Zelene cried. "They're dying. We have to help them!"

Pulling my attention away from the battle, I found my rose. Her face was pinched as if in pain. These were her people. No... *our* people. I brought my hand to her cheek, feeling the soft, hot skin that I had come to know so well during her heat. Her eyes filled with tears, taking on sadness like I'd never seen before. Not even in my father.

"Was it all for nothing?" she whispered. "Did I give you my heart just so you could rip it in two? Make me choose?"

I frowned at her words. *Me*, ripping *her* heart in two? It wasn't like that. I was a king. I had to make the right decision, not the easy one. Every time, without flaw. And if I followed her into a trap the entire pack would pay for it. Fuck me, I'd follow her anywhere, even to my death. But the pack... I swore an oath to protect them.

Just as I swore to be a better king for the

omegas.

Goddamn it.

A tear slipped over the bridge of Zelene's eye and she quickly wiped it away, her expression turning hard. She straightened her shoulders, taking a step back. "If you won't help them," she said, "then I will."

She spun on her heel, running for the stairs.

"Like hell you will," I thundered. My mate wasn't getting anywhere near those beasts. It was my job to protect. Her and everyone else. I would lead my captains and their armies out to help the omegas.

I grabbed Zelene one flight down and pushed her back against the stone wall, pressing my body hard into hers. "You will stay here," I said, finding her eyes. "In the safety of the castle, where a queen belongs. I will do our fighting."

She scowled, shaking her head. "It's too late for that—"

I slammed my mouth down on hers for a brutal kiss. I needed her to know I meant business. That I was still here, still her mate. Still her fucking alpha. I kissed her until she went limp and then pulled back to find her eyes again.

"Stay here," I growled, and hurried off the wall to collect my men.

If this was a mistake, then let it be one made in love. Let them talk about it for years to come. Because nothing had changed. Right or wrong, king or sucker, I loved my omega queen.

FOURTEEN
ZELENE

Like hell would I stay here while those *things* were capturing and destroying omegas.

I hated that I wasn't sure I could trust Adalai to do more than protect his own people. He needed to fight for the omegas. Now. Before he lost their faith forever.

Omegas had been going missing for years. But this was the first sign, the first real proof that it wasn't an accident. Whatever had been done to them, it was for the sole purpose of taking down the Weren. And if the humans hadn't infiltrated the city, they might have gotten away with it. But they wanted to be seen by the king. Simply capturing omegas hadn't gotten the attention of the pack, until now. It was a statement, loud and clear.

The humans intended to win this war. And they would use our own people to do it.

Tavia came skidding around the corner, with Charolet, Rielle, and Ashla close behind. They were out of breath and their pretty hairdos had tumbled from the constraints of their pins.

My sister had her hand on her heart, like she was afraid it would fall out of her chest if she didn't. Or even more urgent, that the mutiny would bring on her shift. Any ordinary alpha marksman in Adalai's army would shoot her first and ask questions never.

"Zee, you know you can't trust him," Charolet said.

"That's not entirely true." I expected four sets of eyes to roll at the declaration. "His mother was an omega. He has omega blood running through his veins. He just has to remember that."

214

"It's Dagger we really have to worry about."
Tavia's gaze shifted to the chaos below us. "If he'd
instituted proper security in the Badlands in the
first place, if he'd taken the missing persons
reports seriously... But it was just omegas
disappearing. So big deal, right? Adalai appointed
someone to defend the Badlands who hates
omegas, and now it's coming back to bite him in
the ass."

My jaw ticked in irritation. She wasn't
familiar enough with Adalai to address him
without his title, even as his sister in law, yet this
wasn't the time for an etiquette lesson. But one
thing was clear. None of them respected the
royals either. It went both ways. If we had any
chance of surviving this battle, we all had to fight
for each other.

Charolet scoffed. "Dagger's freaking out that
the king took an omega queen. Thinks it's a trap.
Funny because I doubt the humans have any idea
how much Dagger hates what he's been assigned
to protect. They don't know that this empire is

one breath away from taking itself out."

"I wonder when he pissed off the king," Rielle added, and then looked to me. "He must have, right? Because the king seems to have some issues about omegas too. Besides you, I mean. Obviously."

We didn't have time for me to give them a history lesson. "Which one of you has worked in the laundry caverns?"

Ashla raised her hand in the back.

"Can you lead us there?" As omegas, we were only allowed in certain areas of the castle. When I worked in the kitchen, I didn't come to the living quarters like Ashla did to bring the king's clean clothes to his wardrobe. As queen, I'd been given a perfunctory tour that excluded the service areas of the castle. It had never felt like more of a handicap.

"Sure." Her forehead wrinkled with doubt. "Only if you tell me why."

"Because we can't kick ass in these dresses, and we need to kick ass. We're headed to the

216

Badlands, to the front lines, because the omegas won't face these beasts alone. Not on my watch."

Their nods of agreement lent me some of the confidence I'd lost.

"Follow me." Ashla turned on her heel and headed down the hallway.

"Zee." Tavia grabbed my shoulder, and the other omegas stopped when they realized we were no longer following them. "You can't just go to the Badlands anymore. You're queen now. You've got a target on your back bigger than any other in this city. Can you imagine how pleased the humans would be if those...*things* captured the omega queen?"

"You sound just like Adalai, thinking I shouldn't fight." I knew she'd hate that, and it might be the only thing that changed her mind. "But I've always had a target on my back. As an omega, I've never been safe. As unmated omega women who go into heat, we live every day in danger of abduction and so much worse. We're not just battling the mutant wolves, Tavia. We're proving to every single person in Luxoria and beyond that omegas are strong, powerful, and worthy of respect."

"I'm not saying you shouldn't do it. Just that we have to take precautions," she muttered as we followed Ashla into the increasingly dark hallways. We'd crossed into omega territory in the castle.

The laundry caverns were in the basement. Dank, damp, and humid, it was one of the most labor intensive omega jobs in the castle. But the caverns also handled the laundry for the King's Battalion. I didn't have to tell Ashla where I wanted her to go. She led us right to a row of perfectly pressed uniform shirts and pants.

"The smaller ones are at the end of the row," she said.

"Grab whatever," I instructed to the ladies. "Where are the boots?" They were shined here too.

"Along the wall."

We'd be at a disadvantage, in clothes and

shoes that were too big for us, but once we shed the beautiful gowns that had seemed like a dream just weeks ago and the jewels we never expected to have access to, we'd blend in with almost any other omega. Or at least, that was what I hoped.

Lucky for us, shields and daggers were also polished in the caverns.

"You can't take those!" The old omega man charged with their care waved his hands, trying to stop us. "You don't belong in here."

"I'm your queen. I'll take what I need." I hated pulling that card on him, but I didn't have time to argue. The man's hands were still in the air when he sank to his knees. "And I'll make sure what's happening in the Badlands, your home, will never happen again after tonight."

"Bless you." His words shook, like he wasn't sure he was doing the right thing.

"I promise you, things will only get better." I took a shield, but the man rose and shook his head.

"This one will work better for you." He

handed me a smaller shield. "The other one is too big, and it will knock you off balance. Hold it over your head and your heart. You shouldn't be fighting, Your Majesty."

"If I don't fight for us, who will?" I didn't miss the tears in his eyes. "Thank you."

The chaos was worse on the ground. Fires burned in the streets, windows were smashed and desperate omegas were taking full advantage of the easy access to goods. When all this was over, I'd make sure they weren't punished. There were too many fist fights, too many men and women who'd gained access to weapons to try to put a stop to it now. I'd only been queen officially for hours, but I already felt like a failure. First, we had to make our city safe from outside forces. Then, once we gave everyone a sense of security, we could work on decades worth of trust issues on the inside.

No guards protected Luxoria from the Badlands tonight. They'd all gone to fight. We slipped into our homeland easily, and my heart broke again when the girls gasped. Nothing was as we left it. The fires were much worse here, and everything was destroyed.

I was frozen in place, my feet screaming from blisters. "The Badlands are destroyed."

"The Badlands are never destroyed," Charolet said. "Omegas get knocked down but we rise again and again. Now let's find and kill these fuckers and show whoever sent them that all their hard work was for nothing."

A roar like a siren rolled over the Badlands. The animalistic sound had come from the mutant beasts. They were nearby. My heart broke knowing they were once omegas like me. We thought the missing ones had been killed. But this was so much worse. They'd been turned into monsters, fighting against themselves and everything they once loved. Now, they would either die, or we would.

It was a lose-lose situation.

I led my army right to the sound. We might have new stolen uniforms, but we'd been fighting for each other for years. I had the utmost confidence in these women. Even more than if I'd been given access to Adalai's entire army. There was no one I'd rather fight with than Tavia, Charolet, Rielle, and Ashla.

That didn't mean I wasn't scared. I was terrified. Lifeless bodies were strewn in the streets with loved ones crouched over them, crying for help. Others charged toward us, urging us to return to the castle.

"Your Majesty, you can't go there," one begged.

"I'm Zelene, just like I have always been. I'm still an omega. I will still fight. I will *always* fight."

I pushed past them, trusting my girls would follow. My promises might have made the omegas feel good when I stood on the castle balcony, with a glittering crown of jewels on my head, but they meant nothing if I didn't fight along with them.

Actions over words.

My heart stopped in my chest when I rounded the next corner. Through the smoke, I met the gaze of one of those horrible mutant beasts. Its eyes were red, and shot little lasers that reflected on my shield. The humans were so confident that none of us could beat their manmade beasts they didn't even try to be subtle.

"Oh, gods," Tavia gasped. "There are so many of them."

I'd been so fixed on the beast with the glowing eyes I didn't see that he had friends. The street was filthy with them, their tangled bodies snarling and hungry. Fur matted and bloody against their flanks. And the smell, like rotting meat and so much spilled blood.

I wanted to puke. I wanted to run. But I couldn't. I was the queen. I had to stand and fight.

I wondered where Adalai was. But it seemed too indulgent to think of him now. I could only hope he was safe.

The first beast, which had to be their alpha, grinned at me, showing off his jagged, broken fangs. A drop of drool darkened the dirt below him, an ominous warning in itself.

Time stopped.

I charged toward the beast, oblivious of the omega's cries for me to stop, trying to remember what the old man told me about the shield. Protect my head and my heart, right?

My sword was pointed right at the mutant wolf. It jerked as it moved, not used to challenge, but it didn't shy away from it. I would break this thing into pieces and send it back to its humans in a box.

But the wolf landed the first blow. He sent me tumbling into the hard earth with a cloud of dirt rising around me. A drop of drool landed on my leg, seeping through my pants. It was way too warm, but I couldn't stop to think about what it was doing to my skin.

I pulled myself up, body screaming, and angled the sword at him. Head, heart...I aimed for his throat, the blade slicing through the air before one of the other wolves caught it in his mouth and pulled it out of my hand.

"Zelene!" My sister yelled, and I cringed.

"She's the queen." The wolf who had drooled on me snickered. "The omega queen. Who would've thunk it. Today's our lucky day."

"Powerless and on the dirty ground before us, just like she should be," another wolf said with a sneer.

One of the girls—I couldn't afford to look back and see which one—tossed her sword at me but it was intercepted before I could reach it. Now I was surrounded by a pack of mutant wolves who would do anything to bring the queen back to their humans.

"Don't you dare hurt her." That was Charolet.

"It will be your turn soon enough, pretty," the mutant alpha chided. "You get a front row seat to see what we'll do to all of you."

One of the wolves took that as an invitation to rip my pant leg. I kicked him right in the face. Bad move, because the other mutants descended, demanding retribution for my sins. My stolen uniform was in tatters, and the alpha sunk his nasty fangs into my thigh...

The last thing I remembered feeling was omega hands on my shoulders, pulling me through the dirt. I wanted to scream but the only people who were coming for me were already here. Adalai was off fighting his own battles.

Adalai.

I hoped if we never saw each other again, he'd remember his promise. To unite the Badlands and let the omegas live in peace.

Silhouettes of wolves were knocked to the ground around me, but I didn't know if that meant I was going to live or die.

I wanted to live. Desperately, wanted to live.

But if it meant revolution for my people... for that, I was ready to die.

FIFTEEN
ADALAI

I roared as my sword sliced through my human enemy's armor. Omega wolves fought beside me, attacking with claws and fangs, while my alpha soldiers battled with sword and shield, and machine guns fired from the city walls. Together, we pushed the humans back from the city gates, but my mind was on the monsters I'd seen from the wall. The half shifted beasts that crushed everything in their path. Where were they?

I already knew the answer.

The Badlands. They must be targeting the

Badlands.

I promised Zelene I would help her people. And I intended to keep that promise.

Calling to Evander and Solen to hold the line at the gate, I fought past quarreling soldiers until the expanse of sand that stretched to the Badlands became dust under my boots. I ran for the largest gathering of people, avoiding the downed bodies. The only way to help them now was to chase the beasts and humans out of their land. Drawing closer, I found Dagger's army fighting in a tight formation, but with the thick smoke in the air, I couldn't see what they battled.

I'd bet it was one of the mangled beasts from earlier.

Terrified omegas ran past me, women and children. Goddamn it, there were children. Of course there were. Why hadn't it mattered to me before? *Didn't think they were in this kind of danger*, my conscience argued, but I couldn't be sure that was the truth. I'd been calloused. Not until Zelene did I understand. Meeting my queen was like pulling blinders from my eyes. I saw everything differently now.

Several humans caught me just outside of the circle but I dispensed of them quickly and rushed into the fray of soldiers and wolves to help. In my head, I could hear the words of the wolves and recognized their voices.

These were Zelene's friends.

Tavia and Charolet and Rielle and Ashla. What the hell were they doing out here?

Shit. My rose would never forgive me if something happened to them. I'd never forgive myself.

I found Dagger, glaring my warnings at him. The Badlands shouldn't have been exposed like this. It was a mistake, another one on my watch. When this was over, he would have to earn back his respect.

Alpha and omega, side by side, we fought the enemy away. But when we closed in on the mutant beasts, it was obvious their attention was focused on something else. They had surrounded something that lay on the ground. They pawed at it, cackling and snorting.

What is it? my animal growled as I fought my way closer, pushing men and wolves out of the way.

And then I saw.

A bloody hand stretched out on the sand. A hand I knew well.

"Zelene!" I roared, my wolf clawing at my chest to be let out. But I had to stay in human form to carry her out of here.

The mutants turned their attention to me. And rightly fucking so. I intended to be the last thing they saw before they lost their heads. Not wasting even a breath, I drove my sword through the nearest beast, slicing him wide. He fell to the ground in a heap, gasping for air. He wouldn't last long.

Twisting, I took on the next one, and the next one while the omega wolves and soldiers pressed in on the humans, until the enemy began to retreat.

When there was no one left to fight, when it was only alphas and omegas, I ran to Zelene. Falling to the ground, I swept her into my arms, furious and terrified at the same time.

"*Rose*. My rose." I shook her gently, and her eyes opened with a start, a vicious snarl in her throat. Her claws poked out from her fingers, slicing across my jaw. Blood trickled hot down my neck as recognition flooded her gaze.

"Adalai?"

"It's me, Zelene. The beasts are gone."

Her eyes closed in relief. "Oh, thank gods."

"What were you doing out here?" I growled and her eyes came open, flashing the same combination of anger and fear I felt myself.

"I... I couldn't sit back and watch. My people were getting hurt. *You* were getting hurt."

"You didn't trust me," I accused.

Shame filled her eyes for a brief moment. "You didn't trust me either."

I sighed, pressing my forehead to hers. "We can't doubt each other anymore. Not if we're going to unite the pack." I knew what we needed. I needed to get her into my bed and finish claiming her. Connect with her like we had in the bunker. Body and soul. Where I could feel her devotion and she could feel mine.

We were the link that bound the two pieces of our pack together. We couldn't let our friends on either side influence what we were building.

"I'm sorry," she whispered so quiet only I could hear her. "I was scared."

"You care more about others than yourself." I couldn't help the edge in my voice. My mate had put herself in danger. What those beasts would have done to her...

"Isn't that what makes a good queen?"

I thought of my mother. The best queen I had ever known. She would have done the same as Zelene. But that didn't mean I had to like it. I pressed her close to my chest, tucking her head under my chin. Her pained gasp brought my attention back to her wounds.

"Where are you hurt?"

She shook her head, trying to sit up. "Just some cuts and scrapes." But the way the lower half of her leg was twisted at an awkward angle told me it was broken.

Dagger ran over, ripping a strip of leather from his jacket. "We need to set it, Your Majesty, before it starts to heal." He knelt beside Zelene and I snarled a low warning. My wolf didn't want him touching her.

"Hey! Hey, you! *Get away from her.*" Tavia's shrill voice pierced the air and she came running over in her human form, naked from her shift. Her fists were clenched as she stared down at Dagger. "Leave her alone."

"I'm trying to help," he argued, shifting his gaze away from her body.

"Haven't you helped quite enough?" Tavia swept her arms wide. "Look at this place. Look what they've done to our home."

"Your home is in the city now," he snapped.

"The Badlands is my home. It will *always* be my home." She lifted her chin. "I am omega."

I watched as his expression changed into something I'd never seen before. Some mixture of regret and bloodlust and resignation. Like he was fighting an internal battle and losing.

Tavia knelt beside Zelene, pushing Dagger out of the way. "It's going to hurt, sister. Like the time you broke your arm, remember?"

Zelene nodded, pressing her lips together.

"I'll make it fast. One... two..." With a swift jerk, Tavia straightened the broken leg.

Zelene let off a strangled cry before swallowing down the agony she must be in. I held her hand while Tavia used a broken branch and Dagger's fabric to tie it off.

"The Queen is hurt. The King fought for us. No, he fought for himself, for her. The Queen risked her life for the Badlands. Lord Dagger fought for us. Lord Dagger is a traitor."

I heard the rumblings around us. The omegas were confused and shaken. My men were as well. The monstrous wolf mutants weren't a foe we were used to dealing with. It was my job to reassure them. To build their trust the same way I did with my mate. The same way I would continue to do, from now until my days as King Alpha came to an end.

I eased Zelene back to the ground and stood to address our people. *My people.* All of them.

"The humans have done something abhorrent to our omegas. Those missing from the Badlands. Your brothers, your friends. Even family. The humans turned them into those vicious beasts. Turned them into weapons to use against us. They did this, knowing our pack was divided, knowing that they could use that division to their benefit. Well, no longer!" I roared. "From this day forward, the Weren are *one*. One pack, one people, under the protection of the King and Luxoria."

An uneasy cheer rose from the crowd. Like they weren't sure if it was a trick. I looked to my alpha soldiers to see many of them nodding in agreement, and I knew things were already moving in the right direction.

But was it enough?

I stared at Dagger. His expression was all over the place. Guilt, sadness, fury. I knew the man. He was my friend. And if I had to guess, I'd say he was sick over what had been done to the Badlands. Once upon a time, he'd taken pride in how strong and resilient the omegas were. None of us had known it was because they could shift or that their unity strengthened them beyond belief. And now, he was partly responsible for what had happened here.

I nodded to myself, understanding what needed to be done. For him, and for the omegas. To redeem his mistakes, and to prove to the Badlands that the kingdom would protect them.

"Dagger." He walked forward, bowing slightly when he stood before me. "You will go in search of the other missing omegas, and bring them home."

He lifted his gaze to mine as shocked gasps arose from the people.

"Your Majesty—"

"You will bring them home before they are turned into the slobbering beasts we fought away today. You will do this... and when you do, you will regain your title. Until then..." I reached forward, ripping the medals from his jacket. "... you are no longer a King's General."

He narrowed his eyes in understanding and bowed his head, submitting to my demands. "Very well, my King." He turned to the omegas he'd been in charge of. "I have let you down," he admitted, his voice hard as rock. "Now, I will see your missing returned." His promise rang into the dark desert night, and I knew Dagger would keep his word or die trying.

I found Zelene's gaze and held it with mine. *See, my Queen? I will choose you, choose* us. *Every fucking time.*

She nodded, as if she heard me, and her eyes shone with love. A million enemies couldn't crush what I felt for her. But let them try.

SIXTEEN
ZELENE

Tavia threw up her hands and shook her head when she walked into my bedroom. "You can't stay still, can you?"

I'd only gone from the bed to the chair. No lie, I was going a little stir crazy, and at least from the chair I had a view of the castle gardens. Everything slowed down when I watched the Joshua trees sway in the breeze in time with the gorgeous blooms below them. The desert roses that made me think of Adalai.

"When was the last time you spent all day in bed while people waited on you hand and foot?"

Another shake of her head, and she gave me one of those looks only sisters could give each other. "Let's see...never."

"Exactly. And let me tell you how much you'd suck at it."

"You're supposed to be recovering. And if you keep hobbling around on that broken leg, it won't heal right."

Taking time to heal was a luxury that we'd never been afforded in the Badlands. Good thing our inner animals could expedite the healing process. If I didn't have a leg in a cast, I'd take serious issue to having Tavia wait on me, like she was still a servant. But the truth was, my broken leg hurt like hell and as a brand new queen with mutant wolves on the loose, I didn't feel comfortable slipping away from reality for long. I'd even refused the painkillers that were offered to me.

Truly, I wanted my sister here with me. She made the transition from omega to royalty feel normal, and she was still feisty enough to ask the questions I might have missed.

"I'll be back in heels in no time," I assured her. "Have you thought about what you want your new role to be once you don't have to take care of your invalid sister?"

She grinned, and took the seat across from me. Her gaze was drawn out the window too. The riot of color would never not be special to us. "It's an honor to take care of the queen, no matter what my status is. It's even more important now, because we have power. If I may presume that Her Majesty will listen to counsel."

I rolled my eyes. "I'm still Zelene, no matter where I live or what my job is."

"I know that, but some conversations have to be had with the queen. This is one of them."

"What's wrong?" I wasn't naive enough to think once we secured the city from mutant threats, and the missing omegas were safety returned to the Badlands, we'd be able to rest. Even if there were no more threats to the city, we had so much healing to do. So much to learn about each other. It was why it was so important to have Tavia and the rest of the ladies here with me. Not only would they keep things painfully real, they'd never let me forget where I came from.

When it was just Adalai and me, it was easy to get lost in the clouds.

Tavia braced herself. Her shoulders curved forward, and she folded her hands together in her lap. Whatever she had to tell me made her nervous.

"I'm concerned about Dagger being assigned to bring the omegas back."

"You've always had a problem with Dagger." She'd been in opposition of his Badlands leadership for years. I always worried that her strong opinions would get her in trouble. Now I was certain of it. "Adalai disciplined him, and if he didn't think he was capable of doing the job, he wouldn't send him to do it. No alpha knows more about the Badlands and what happens there than Dagger."

I knew that wasn't enough for my sister.

242

"Adalai won't give him back his title until the Badlands are safe. Even if the wellbeing of the omegas isn't important to him yet, we know his title matters a lot."

Tavia took a moment to digest what I said, but it sent a shiver down her spine. "I can't trust him that easily. Without supervision, he can report anything to Adalai. Just like you'd take my word at face value, I believe Adalai will do the same for Dagger. Not because he's a weak leader. He trusts his people, which is a good thing. Until it isn't."

"You think that someone should go with him." I thought about how I'd propose sending a babysitter along with Dagger. Even though Tavia often jumped to the worst case scenario, she was right. Dagger needed a skilled team, and I'd suggest Adalai send an omega representative with him. There were things that we saw every day that alphas would miss because they would never have that sort of familiarity with the Badlands.

"I'm going with him." Her gaze met mine. She

wasn't asking permission.

"Like hell you are, Tavia." I swore to myself I'd never pull the queen card on any of my girls, but that promise faded as soon as my sister declared she intended to co-lead a revolution with Adalai's very skilled, very disgraced, and probably very pissed off right-hand man.

"What should I do, stay here and play dress up with you while I do something meaningless in the castle and pretend our people aren't disappearing and being turned into mutant lab animals?" Her mouth settled in a hard line. "The view is gorgeous here, Zelene, but it doesn't change the fact that beyond these flowers, people are suffering. You used to be one of them. If you weren't the one wearing the crown, you'd be out there on the front lines, demanding justice for every omega in the Badlands."

That was a punch to the gut. "I will be out there on the front lines, every day, for all the people of Luxoria. Minutes ago you were begging me to take the time to heal. This is new to me. I'm doing the best I can."

"I know." Tavia stood and rounded my chair, and picked up my hair. I loved that. It was how she'd calmed me down so many nights, when the Badlands was hell on earth. When I was the one with the crazy ideas, and she had to talk me out of them. "You're doing an amazing job."

"So what's your plan?" I turned back to catch her face light up when she realized I was going along with it, whatever it was.

"Not sure yet, besides holding Dagger accountable at absolutely every turn." That grin was wicked. "And making sure that everyone in Luxoria and beyond never forgets how powerful omegas can be."

We startled when the door opened. We weren't expecting company.

"Apologies, my rose. Tavia." Adalai nodded at my sister. "I'm still not used to having someone waiting for me when I come home."

That turned me into a puddle of goo. Even Tavia softened. Someday, she'd learn to trust the alphas. Maybe sending her to accompany Dagger would be good for her too. She'd have to work with him, and maybe she'd stop thinking of him as an enemy.

Tavia curtsied to Adalai. "Her Majesty is healing nicely. But she's having a hard time staying in one place."

Adalai grinned. "Our queen has never been one for following rules."

"I can hear you guys," I groaned.

Tavia gave me a quick peck on the cheek. "I'll leave you two alone. I'm sure you have plenty to talk about."

Right, like the fact she'd just installed herself as Dagger's right-hand woman. But I had news too. Something I had yet to share with anyone.

Adalai waited until the door clicked closed, and then turned to me with an amused grin. "What are the two of you cooking up?"

I placed my hand over my heart and feigned surprise. "What would ever make you think we were up to something?"

"I'd be more disappointed if you weren't." He was down on one knee beside me, and our lips met in a kiss. A surrender of all that once was.

"Tavia wants to go with Dagger to find the humans that are turning omegas into mutants." I said it fast, when he was still drunk from the kiss.

Adalai didn't reply right away. "It's not a horrible idea."

Maybe I was the intoxicated one. "Really?"

"It will show anyone who questions our union, and the end of The Division, that we're serious about equality." Mischief flickered in the king's eyes. "And she'll definitely teach Dagger a few lessons that I can't."

That was what I loved about Adalai. He was able to admit that he was only as good as his team. "You're going to make an amazing dad."

His eyes widened. I slapped my hand over my mouth and then pulled it away fast. "Did I say that out loud?"

"You did." He moved in front of me, careful not to bump my leg as he took my hands in his.

"My rose, are you pregnant with my child?"

My grin couldn't be contained. I nodded, accepting his lips on mine. This kiss was pure celebration. Adoration. A war could rage right outside our window, and those beautiful blooms could turn angry and violent, and I would feel safe because I was in his arms.

"Soon we'll have a prince, and he'll never know a Luxoria that was divided." It was the perfect fairy tale I wanted to read to my children. "He'll only know love, acceptance, and opportunity."

"And he'll be strong and brave because his mother is the queen who challenged everything." He gave me another kiss. "The one that returned Luxoria to glory, as our own mothers knew it. They're smiling on us, my rose. They're proud."

I'd never been surer that I'd done the right thing, sneaking into the party that night. It seemed like another lifetime. I would make everyone proud, especially my king, no matter what it took.

As he kissed me again, I knew this was exactly where I was meant to be. *Who* I was meant to be.

His.

His queen.

His forbidden omega.

And he was mine.

Thank you for reading

HIS FORBIDDEN OMEGA.

We hope you enjoyed Adalai and Zelene's
story as much as we enjoyed writing it!

Read on for a sneak peek of
Dagger and Tavia's story,
the next book in
The Royal Omegas!

DAGGER

I stood in the middle of The Badlands—what was left of it—and let my gaze take in the reality before me. It was in ruins. The bright desert sun gleamed overhead, highlighting every demolished shanty, the charred fences, destroyed goods that inhabitants had tucked away for desperate days. With or without the sun, my eyes couldn't avoid the people who milled about, seeming lost.

Lost. Did I look lost to them too?

This land that bordered Luxoria to the south was home to the omegas, the lowest class of shifters among the Weren people.

No. Not the lowest. Not anymore.

Not since King Adalai took an omega as queen and declared The Division null and void.

No more segregation, no more pack divided. We were now one. Alpha, beta, and omega alike.

I should have been happy about it, like so many others were. Like Evander and Cassian. Even Solen wasn't pissing in the king's mead over this. And there was a certain feel among the city these days. Lighter, even if omegas were still getting side-eyed.

But I wasn't happy about any of it.

There was a place for everything and everyone. The omegas' place was in The Badlands. Mine was... used to be... at the king's side. Commander of the Southern Border. Overseer of The Badlands. Not anymore. With my title stripped, I was just another alpha vying for a place in this world. I had nothing and no one now.

Except my mission.

King Adalai was sending me on a quest to find the omegas who had been abducted from the

Badlands over the past years. I was no stranger to hearing of these missing persons complaints, but I'd never taken them seriously. The Badlands was... well, bad. It made sense that desperate shifers might try to leave in search of something better. They wouldn't find it. Anyone with any sense knew that beyond the desert there was only more desert.

And humans. There were humans who wanted things from us. Wanted to exploit our abilities and experiment on us to their own gain. Humans who wanted our technology so they could thrive in the world as it was now, after the Great Dust Storm that sent humanity into chaos.

Luxoria was an oasis everyone wanted a piece of. It made sense that the desperate omegas who called The Badlands home, might have gone in search of another place like it.

I knew now, that wasn't the case.

Omegas had been taken, one at a time, for years by the humans who turned them into living weapons. Twisted versions of their former selves, half shifted beasts who drooled acid and sliced wolves in half with their claws.

They had come to destroy The Badlands, and did a pretty fine job of it. The only good thing about that night was that none of the mutants returned to the humans alive.

But the number of missing omegas was nearly in the triple digits. Which meant there were plenty more mutants—or soon-to-be mutants—in the humans' arsenal. It was up to me to find them before they met that fate.

It was part punishment for my role in the Badlands destruction, part rescue mission. The alpha in me bucked against taking any ounce of blame, but the king and others felt I'd neglected my duties. Easy for them to say, when they were in charge of betas and other alphas. I'd been tasked with policing the omegas. The lawless, the forgotten. The trash no one cared about. No one could understand the situation my assignment put me in.

If I'd cared too much, my loyalty to the crown

would have been questioned.

If I cared too little... well, that was where I was at now.

The balance I'd had to keep was narrow and impossible, but my true feelings laid somewhere in the middle. At times, I related more to the omegas than my own class. At times, I hated the alphas as much as they did.

Hated myself.

For living on the other side of the gates while people suffered, deservingly or not. For knowing children starved while the royals ate their fill. For never reporting these things to the king, whether he would have cared then or not.

For watching an omega female and wishing she could be mine.

I went still as I spotted her across a great distance, blinking twice to make sure it was really her. She wasn't dirty like the first time I saw her in the castle. And though her dress was bland now, it wasn't ratted and torn like before. Her dark hair was braided back against her head, but it wasn't caked in mud this time.

Tavia was different now that her sister was queen, but she still liked to pretend she was one of the desperate. She'd made me hate myself the most, and didn't even know it. Never would, if I had anything to say about it.

Pulling my eyes away from her, I focused on the horizon.

The omegas had become my people without ever meaning to. I was The Division, half dedicated to them, and half to my king. The barrier between them and the city. It had been my darkest and most tightly kept secret, and would remain as such until the day I died.

What the fuck was I now? Where did I belong in this new unified pack that King Adalai vied for?

None of those feelings the omegas brought out in me mattered more than my station. My place.

Now, I had to earn it back.

I would leave at dawn. I'd find every omega lost on my watch, and bring them home. And while I was at it, I'd find myself. Never again would I be torn between honor and duty.

Never again.

***

TAVIA

Becoming the first omega queen in a generation wasn't even close to the most reckless thing my sister Zelene had ever done. Keeping her ass out of hot water was a part time job, and I never dared tell her that it was the reason I got fired from my position at the castle. The first one, anyway. At the time, it seemed like the end of the world.I thought it was a secret I'd take to my grave. If I wasn't good enough to work for the Luxoria royal family, no one else would hire me. I couldn't put her job in jeopardy. We would've starved to death.

But the spark in her eyes when she cooked up trouble had sometimes been the only light in The Badlands,

Now here we were, in the private suite of the

royal castle in Luxoria. No, we weren't trespassing. We lived here now. Zelene did, anyway, now that she was mated to King Adalai.

My sister was an actual queen. I still had trouble wrapping my head around it.

That was why, despite Zelene's protests, I went home to the Badlands every night. Omegas had been sentenced to a life of misery there, so the former king could settle a score. Adalai's father.

The former king had fallen in love with an omega too. But it didn't stop him from bringing us so much misery.

For that reason, I would never trust Adalai or anyone in his court. Bloodthirsty and ruthless, they would do anything to save their own asses. After twenty five years in The Badlands, I understood survival instinct more than I ever wanted to. The difference between the Alphas and me? I wouldn't put someone else in harm's way to save myself.

Now, it was my turn to be the reckless one.

"As queen, I can forbid you from going."

Zelene hugged a velvet pillow to her chest. Her broken leg relegated her to the suite. She had crutches, but she refused to show weakness. Everyone in the city and beyond had their eyes on the omega queen. Her favorite seat was by the window, overlooking the garden. Beyond that, we could see the Badlands. Some might say she was hiding, but she was the first line of defense in another attack.

"You'd forbid me from going back to the Badlands? How soon you forget where you came from." I scoffed. She swore she never would.

"It's not safe. It never was, but especially not now. The mutants will be looking for you, specifically, because the humans would love nothing more than to capture the sister of the queen." She shuddered, and the same chill went down my spine. "So yes, I can command you to stay here. Or I'll..."

She had nothing.

"How will you punish me that's worse than what we already lived through?" I looked to the door, to make sure the King hadn't paid us a surprise visit. He did that, a lot. It was probably supposed to be romantic, sneaking up on his new bride, but I didn't know much about that lovey dovey stuff. To me it felt like he was checking up on us.

"If you get caught, there's no telling what will happen to you." Zelene shuddered as a host of possibilities went through her head. They were certainly going through mine. "The humans already treated omegas like lab rats. If they can get their hands on you..."

"I don't trust Dagger will come back with the living omegas. He'll cut a deal with the humans to get what he wants, not what's best for the Badlands. He's never done right by us."

Until Adalai stripped Dagger of his duties and title, he'd been in charge of keeping the Badlands safe.For five years, he'd ensured our lives were a living hell. Now he promised he'd turn a new leaf, and do the right thing. I'd believe it when I saw it. When all the missing omegas came back to the

Badlands safe.

"You have to trust Dagger," Zelene said, and I had no idea how she kept a straight face. That man was as much our enemy as the humans that captured omegas and turned them into mutant wolves.

I wouldn't let the crown change my sister. I'd do whatever it took to keep her true to her roots.

"You don't trust Dagger to keep me safe."

She pursed her lips together, and for the first time since the crown had been placed on top of her head, she looked vulnerable. Not weak. No omega was weak. Especially not our queen. But every once in a while, our walls came crashing down. It was impossible to keep them up all the time.

"No, I don' trust him," she said. "I think he'll do whatever Adalai asks of him to get his title back. But that's where it ends. He'll see you as a challenge, Tavia. And more than that, a representation of all his failures. Dagger couldn't impose his will on the Badlands. Especially not on us. As much as he tried, he couldn't make us submit. He'll expect you to fight for yourself."

"I've been fighting for my life every damn day." Since omegas had been exiled from Luxoria. If Dagger thought I'd give up easily, that I'd stop fighting just because my sister slept in the King's bed, he had another think coming. "I'm ready."

About the Authors

P. Jameson likes to spend her time daydreaming, and then rearranging those dreams into heartstring-pulling stories of trial and triumph. Paranormal is her jam, so you're sure to find said stories full of hot alpha males of the supernatural variety. She lives next door to the great Rocky Mountains with her husband and kids, who provide her with plenty of writing fodder.

Kristen Strassel is far cooler than she'll make herself sound in this bio. She enjoys spending time with the voices in her head—nudging the characters toward those bad decisions and seeing if she can get them a happily ever after. When she's not writing, she's often still in the land of make-believe—doing makeup for film and television. And when she's not doing any of that, she enjoys making her house look like a Pinterest board, watching football, and road trips to the middle of nowhere

Made in the USA
Coppell, TX
02 September 2021

61641799R00148